CHRISTINE DORÉ MILLER

Evernight Teen ®

www.evernightteen.com

CHRISTINE DORÉ MILLER

If you or someone you know is in an abusive relationship, or if you have questions about abuse, please call 1-866-331-9474 or visit **www.loveisrespect.org**

CHRISTINE DORÉ MILLER

 FORGIVEN ARE THE STARRY-EYED

Christine Doré Miller

Copyright © 2019

Chapter One

My eyelids closed as if they were being drawn down by sluggish, unhurried weights. When I forced them open after several seemingly endless moments, nothing had changed. I could still make out a blurry image of Josh standing nearby, Mr. Thompson's hands clenched firmly on Josh's shoulders from behind. There was a crowd, I think, and muffled voices. The steel school locker felt cold against my back and I recognized the familiar feeling that lately seemed to just dwell and ache in my bones. Fear, I think it was, mixed with just enough madness to keep the blood racing through my veins … fast. Too fast.

"Why did you do that, Andrea?" Josh shouted in my direction.

My eyes fell closed again. I don't remember what else he said. I just remember the feeling of each overly pronounced syllable piercing the air while he said it. I stared through the darkness that danced behind my heavy eyelids. What had I done?

I tried to pry open my hazy eyes to examine the faces of the expanding crowd as they stood, mouths agape. I only recognized a few. There were hardcover music books sprawled open on the tile floor at my feet. Confused, I looked to Josh, but the heavy silence of the room deafened any words he may have been saying. I gripped the ends of my soft, thin hair between my slender fingers and waited. Each thought sunk deeper than the last.

There was a poster taped sloppily against the locker behind me. I turned my head to face it and focused. The ends were curled up and there were ripples in the masking tape adorned to the edges. "Oakwood High School Invitational—TONIGHT" it read in handwritten purple block letters. There was a pixelated saxophone image pasted underneath the words, "Brought to you by Mr. Thompson and the Oakwood High Jazz Band." I brought my hand up to trace the edges. The poster board felt crisp and thick under my fingertips. I could smell the aftermath of the permanent marker. The loud reverberating voice behind me got softer until it resembled a deep echo I could easily ignore. I started to pick at the tape from the bottom left corner of the poster until I felt the sticky residue ball up underneath my fingernail.

Suddenly the life reentered my body in one abrupt breath when I felt a strong tug on my arm. I turned and saw Ethan Marks. Everyone else was gone. Had it been minutes this time? Hours?

"Andrea! Come on," he barked at me, interlacing my arm, tucking it quickly under his. He jerked me to a standing position and pulled me down the hall, speeding up his gate as I stumbled to catch up.

"Where's Josh?" I asked worriedly, but he didn't answer. We were silent as we walked through the empty hallway. I lifted my gaze, trying to catch Ethan's eye, trying to read his thoughts. His light blue eyes, usually sparkling with laughter, were steely and somber as he charged forward, dragging me with him, away from the wreckage I'd caused.

He stopped short and took a deep breath. His eyes were unyielding and dismal as they studied me, and slowly his frustration melted into a deep sadness.

"What happened, Andrea? What was that back there?"

"I don't know..." My voice began breaking. My thoughts were muddled beyond recognition and I couldn't form the right words, or any words, to explain.

Ethan wrapped himself around me in a gentle, firm embrace. It felt kind. And warm. And wonderfully different. My muscles unclenched for the first time in months, and I didn't know I was crying until I tasted the salt as it stained my face. I buried my head into Ethan's chest as he tightened his hold on me. I wanted him to say something, to tell me everything would be all right, but we both knew better. So we just stood there, Ethan supporting me as I clasped the back of his cotton t-shirt between my fingers.

After a few minutes, I fully returned to my body as my breathing calmed. I steadied my stance and took a step backward, shakily holding Ethan's forearms as I regained my balance. Wiping smudged mascara from my pale face, I met Ethan's eyes and quickly looked down, fixating on a crack in the tile below me.

"Hey," he started, "Andrea ... it's..."

"I'm okay. Ethan, I'm sorry. I'm sorry you had to ... I'm sorry I ... ugh your shirt." I motioned to the tear stains on his light green tee that crept from his chest to his shoulder.

"Oh God, don't worry about that. Andie, I just..."

"It's fine." I wiped my face and took a deep breath. "Thanks," I said, squeezing Ethan's hand and looking in his eyes sincerely, so he knew I meant it. "I should go. But thanks." I shook my head and turned around to walk back into the havoc and face what I had done. I felt Ethan staring at me as I left. He was just another person whose life would've been better if he hadn't met me. I swallowed, took a breath, and kept walking.

It was over for now, that latest incident, and there was no way to tell when there would be another one … but there would definitely be another one. I was too broken for it to be any other way.

After walking a short distance, I finally recognized Josh amidst dozens of hurried students and parents milling toward the cafeteria. I meekly smiled and gave a half wave, unsure of how he'd be feeling after what had just happened, unsure if he'd even want to see me. But I was drawn toward him like the strongest magnet, unable to stay away no matter how much I resisted or how much damage I'd caused.

"Come on, babe, we've only got an hour until we have to be back at the awards ceremony," Josh said, his dark brown eyes transfixed on me with concern. He didn't mention the incident. I didn't either.

Josh's words were soft, but I couldn't shake the horror from my body. How could he still love me after this? He deserved better. Everyone did.

Josh motioned for me to follow him outside the double doors that led to the parking lot. As the cold Michigan air hit my face, I went to grab Josh's hand. He quickly dropped it when he saw Harper and jogged to catch up with her. I tried to follow briskly but was still carefully avoiding the ice patches on the black asphalt as I heard a car start.

"Come on, slowpoke!" Harper teased from the driver's seat. I piled into the backseat of her 1980s white hatchback and had barely buckled my seatbelt before we started moving.

Chapter Two

It wasn't always like this, with so much despair lingering in the electric air, though it seemed like the good moments were becoming fewer and the incidents were lasting longer as time went on.

I met Josh in Autumn. It was the beginning of my junior year, and the leaves had just started changing. My best friend Harper Cooley and I walked into the school band rehearsal room after class one day to see an unfamiliar boy seated at the piano. He had dark, messy hair and tired, soulful eyes. When he stood up, it looked as if he'd walked out of a 70's poster, donning a tie dye Hendrix t-shirt, faded brown corduroys, and a beaded hemp bracelet.

"Andrea! Harper!" I heard Ethan's voice from across the room. "Hey, lovely," he said, giving me a quick side hug. Ethan was a drummer, and always had sticks hanging out of his baggy cargo khakis, which I heard clack together when he hugged me. We bonded our freshman year over our love for sad music, indie movies, and dark humor. We'd been close ever since. "Have you guys met Josh McMillan yet? He's a goddamn monster on the piano. We are so lucky to have him." Ethan motioned to the stranger behind the keys.

"Hi," Josh said, giving me an understated smile that made my heart flutter. He didn't look like anyone I had seen in our small Midwest town before. I took a step closer and bit my lip, hiding the smile that was giving me away.

"Hey, I'm Andrea. I guess I'm the new student conductor," I said, while looking down at the scuff marks on my black ankle boots.

"You guess? Oh please," said Ethan. "Andrea's a

rockstar. She's our new director because she was too badass back at the percussion station. Mr. Thompson thought she deserved a promotion."

"Ha ha, Ethan," I snapped, embarrassed at the attention, but secretly thrilled that he made me look good in front of the new, cute pianist. "This is Harper, lead saxophone." I waved in her direction.

She awkwardly reached her hand out for a shake, and Josh laughed.

"A little formal, yeah? Ok, I'll bite." He shook her hand.

Harper's face turned redder than usual.

As practice got underway, we all had a front-row ticket to Josh's astonishing talent. He was a master. I'd never seen a teenager play like that. Or an adult for that matter. His artistry was so free, so passionate, so beautiful. It was stunning to watch and hard to tear my eyes away from the keyboards while I attempted to focus on the other sections. I could tell Ethan was annoyed, but I didn't care. I was hooked.

When practice ended, Harper and I headed outside, hoping to catch another glimpse of Josh before we left. Disappointed when I didn't see him nearby, I was taken aback when I suddenly saw him running toward us. Jumping high, he slapped the top of the door frame, turned around, and gave me a quick wink.

"Bye ladies," he said as he hopped into his maroon sedan with a Beatles sticker adorned to the bumper.

"Holy shit," I said, having not meant for that to be out loud.

"I know, right?" said Harper. "God he's *hot*."

Ugh, I thought to myself. Harper was interested, too. This was probably going to end up off-limits, and we'd see Josh end up dating one of those girls that Harper and I hated. We playfully called their squad "Kid A" because they always wore tight Radiohead shirts to school and mini-skirts with studded belt buckles, but Nicole, their leader, legitimately thought "Kid A" was a Dr. Seuss character until Harper embarrassingly corrected her in the cafeteria.

"You're thinking of Thing 1, dumbass," Harper had said when she overheard Nicole's conversation. "*Kid A* is the best Radiohead album of all time, but you're too fake to know that."

"Whatever, hater," Nicole replied, rolling her eyes. Despite their lack of knowledge for anything truly alternative or interesting, Nicole and the Kid A squad played a good game and filled out those shirts better than we ever could. Those girls always won. Even Ethan dated one, and he was one of the good guys. Harper and I prided ourselves on being unique, but for all the *right* reasons. We told each other and ourselves that we didn't care what other people thought, but in the same breath we'd painstakingly analyze and agonize over every Instagram comment we'd receive. Both of our cars were covered in political and punk rock stickers while the Kid A girls drove pristine SUVs. We spent our weekends making the hour-long trek to Detroit for underground ska concerts while they had soccer practice and hosted elaborate parties with alcohol that their slightly older siblings bought with fake IDs. We were never invited, but we pretended it didn't bother us. Harper and I had each other, and that always felt like enough.

You would never know Harper had such a bold palette just by looking at her. She appeared painfully plain. Forgettable. Her wispy straw-colored hair fell limp by her pink, freckled face. She was terribly unfeminine, a little pudgy, and had a very meek voice, even though she had a lot to say. Her lips were thin, her nose was long, and her brow often furrowed while she thought. But God, she was cool. When you got her talking, you wouldn't want her to stop. She was the smartest person I knew. Not only did she excel in every AP class the school offered, but she just knew so much about the world, which was rare for this small town. She spoke Spanish, was a regular at the only Indian restaurant in the city and planned to travel the world after college. I admired Harper. She was a year older than me, and I was terrified of what my senior year would look like without her. I was afraid she'd meet equally interesting co-eds at the University of Michigan, where she'd gotten early acceptance, while I'd be stuck in the school cafeteria, listening to Ethan drone on about his hatred for electronic music for the thousandth time.

"And did you hear him play?" Harper asked, referring to Josh. "I mean ... wow. He's kind of incredible."

"Yeah, it was hard to concentrate!" I giggled.

"It's about time we got some hotties at this school. I wonder if he has a girlfriend?"

"Why? Are you gonna try and talk to him?" I already knew the answer but hoped I was wrong.

"Hell yeah. Unless ... you're interested?"

"Well yeah! But don't worry, I'll stay away if you want to go for it." Neither Harper or I had ever had a real boyfriend. I had a kissed a guy my freshman year at a home football game, but he ended up dating a Kid A crony. Such was my life. So besides that quick brush with romance that lasted all of one night, I was a complete newbie. Harper hadn't even had her first kiss yet. She talked a big game, but I knew her secrets. She'd had plenty of crushes, but guys didn't typically return her fervor. I think it bothered her more than she let on.

"No, no ... sisters before misters, right?" she said,

forcing a smile. "Kid A will swallow him up anyway, so what's the point? He's cool, though. We should still try and hang with him."

"Thanks, Harp. Just think, next year you'll be at U of M, surrounded by guys like that."

"Well, I can't argue with that." She smiled. "Come on, let's get out of here."

Chapter Three

The next week, Harper and I made it our mission to plug Josh into our group of friends. We said it was because we wanted to take advantage of having someone so new and exciting at our school, but I think deep down we knew better. We both liked him. And the more time we spent with him, the closer we'd get. Closer to what, we weren't sure, but even if nothing happened, it was just exhilarating to be near him.

When Ethan announced he was going to have a game night, I practically begged him to let us invite Josh. Once Ethan agreed, Harper quickly volunteered to be the one to extend the invitation.

I watched the minutes tick off the clock during final period that day, my mind fixated on Josh. Would he say yes? He'd probably say yes. But what if he said no? What if he laughed? When I finally saw Harper after school, I felt my stomach knot up until she flashed me a thumbs up, and I finally let out a relieved breath.

"So he's coming?" I asked quickly as she got closer.

"You know it!"

"Awesome! How did the conversation go?" I wanted to hear every detail.

"Well.." She let out a short sigh. "I told Josh about the game night, and then he asked if *you* were going. So I said yeah, and then he said he'd come."

"What? Really?" I felt myself blush. Harper seemed less than pleased that Josh had asked about me, but I couldn't hide my smile. "Cool," I said, trying to sound normal. I didn't know what his comment meant exactly, but I knew it felt good. I tried not to think about what complications could arise if he were *actually* interested in me, so I just reminded myself that I wasn't the type of girl that new, exotic strangers found attractive. Not when people like Nicole and Kid A roamed the halls. Why would Josh pick me, the band geek with an early curfew, when there were prettier, cooler girls to choose from who put out and smoked pot? He was probably just being polite. Or maybe he liked my personality. That's what usually happened. Guys would label Nicole as "hot" and me as "nice." I hated being "nice."

By the time Ethan's game night rolled around, I had, after dozens of tries, finally picked out the perfect outfit. I wanted to look casual but not forgettable, so while I wore my standard Pixies t-shirt, skinny jeans, and Vans slip-ons. I paired it with a flashy red cardigan and rosy eyeshadow to give it a little extra something. This way I'd still look like myself so nobody could say I was trying too hard, but hopefully my bright accent choices would also show Josh that I'm more than just a pair of checkered Vans and hair dye.

When Harper picked me up that night to head to Ethan's, I did a double take when I got in the car. I had never seen Harper in makeup before. Her bright blue eyeshadow was scrawled messily across her lids, and her blush just made her pink face even pinker. It looked like a child had applied it. I wanted to help her, but I thought she'd be offended if I admitted she looked ridiculous. So I let it go, but not mentioning it felt like there was a pink-cheeked elephant in the room as we drove to Ethan's house. I knew she was trying to impress Josh, but I didn't have the heart to tell her she was probably doing the opposite.

When we got there, Josh had already arrived. He and Ethan were playing video games in the basement when we entered down the stairs.

"Hey, ladies," Ethan announced, keeping his eyes glued to the TV screen.

"Yes! I *owned* you!" Josh exclaimed as he dropped his controller in an apparent victory.

"Goddammit," Ethan said. "You suck!"

"Where is everyone?" I asked, referring to our other friends from the jazz band who usually joined.

"On the way," Ethan replied as he stood up.

"Well, now that the always lovely Miss Cavanaugh is here, the party can begin," Josh said toward me as he walked closer and playfully grabbed my hand and nudged me into a twirl. I laughed and saw Harper tense up from the corner of my eye.

"What's up, Harp," Josh said.

"Oh, not much," she said, walking closer, trying to place herself in his line of vision, but he kept his eyes on me. I felt my skin itch when he stared at me and I couldn't get my feet to stop awkwardly tapping, but the excitement that was slowly welling up in my chest made the discomfort easier to tolerate.

As the night progressed and the others arrived, we spent most of our time in laughter. It was the most fun I'd had in a long time. Josh seemed to fit right in with our humor, and even Harper finally relaxed during the second round of Pictionary. Every time we played a game that involved teams, Josh demanded that we be paired together. His interest became so apparent that even Ethan called him out on it.

"Geeze, get a room you two," he said when Josh picked me for the third time in a row.

I was mortified, but Josh just laughed it off.

"Trust me, dude, I wouldn't mind." He nudged my arm with his elbow. I couldn't tell how much he was joking. But I was pretty sure this was how flirting felt. I had no clue what an appropriate response would be, so when in doubt, I just smiled.

I didn't talk much that night. I didn't have to. Even though Harper and Josh bonded over their love for The Doors and David Bowie, he stayed focused on me. While they playfully argued about who the best Beatle was, he rested his hand on my knee. And when they joked with each other about some Janis Joplin reference I didn't understand, he kept looking over even though I tried to appear occupied by talking with Ethan.

When the night ended, Josh gave Harper a high five and then came toward me and opened his arms wide. He embraced me in a big bear hug that made my knees buckle, but I felt Harper's eyes burning into me from behind, so I pulled away quickly.

"Oh man, Ethan, look at this, no love from Andie," Josh said with a smile. "Don't worry. I'll win you over." He winked.

I blushed and looked down.

"All right, let's get you home before your curfew," Harper said snottily, but I didn't care. Even her jealousy couldn't ruin my high that night.

Chapter Four

After a few weeks had gone by, Josh had officially become one of us. The school was buzzing with rumors and insights on the new, weird kid who played piano like a god. I was proud that we claimed him first, and had so far kept him away from the grips of Kid A.

Josh, Harper, Ethan, and I had even hung out a few times after band rehearsal. It was exhilarating to be around Josh. His energy was infectious, and every once in a while, I'd catch him looking at me, but when I would meet his gaze, he never looked away. He'd just smile as if he wanted me to know he'd been staring. I would get a palpable buzz off those glimpses. Maybe knowing he was off limits raised the thrill factor, but his charm, his magnetism, was just invigorating. I'd never met someone so carefree, who said whatever was on their mind. He seemed fearless, and I couldn't get enough.

Sometimes Josh would slip around our group texts to send me a few candid words privately. I saved his messages in a hidden folder on my phone, and when nobody was around, I'd pour through them and feel myself draw deeper into his allure.

"Good morning beautiful" was one of my favorites, followed closely by "thinking about you when I should be thinking about math—get out of my head okay?" I knew I was playing with fire by enabling this flirtation. Harper would be crushed if she found out. But I rationalized it by reminding myself that who Josh liked was Josh's decision, not mine. And I prepared talking points in my head in case things ever escalated, or Harper got a stronger whiff of our seemingly mutual attraction.

"I can't help that he likes me," I would say. "It all

just happened so fast."

I knew I was not acting like a good friend, but every time I'd wake up with the intention to end our playful exchanges, he'd do something sweet, and I'd get sucked back in. He even made me custom playlists, first of bands he thought I'd like, and then of songs he said made him think of me. "Magic" by Ben Folds Five, "Maybe I'm Amazed" by Paul McCartney, and "I Want You" by The Beatles were the first three songs on that mix, and before the fourth even started, I was hooked, swept away, and quickly replaced my internal debate about friendship with rehearsing what seemed like an inevitable awkward conversation I'd need to have with Harper.

One day after band practice, as everyone packed up their instruments and headed to the parking lot, Josh pulled me aside. I held my breath when he touched my arm, turning me toward him.

"Hey you," he said, his eyes filled with a mystery I was dying to crack. "We haven't gotten to spend too much time together, just you and me. Do you want to come over? I can show you that Pavement album I was telling you about."

"Oh, um, sure," I said, remembering my parents wouldn't be home from work until after 6 PM. "I'll grab Harper and Ethan." I started to turn.

"No, Andrea. I uh ... I was just thinking you and me."

"Oh, um ... yeah okay, I'll follow you in my car." The words came out before I had thought them through.

Not cool, I thought. *You know better*. But the thrill I felt run through my body at the thought of having alone time with Josh outweighed my sense of loyalty, and I slipped out the door before I ran into Harper.

I drove behind Josh while we winded through the

side streets until we reached his house, an expensive ranch-style home tucked behind the golf course of the local country club. My heart was pounding the entire drive. I parked on the street and followed him as he unlocked the front door. Walking into the living room, it was not at all what I expected. There were pristine white carpets, ceramic statues, ivory wall treatments, and professional family photos placed near the overstuffed white leather couch.

"Wow," I said, as Josh threw his backpack by the front door.

"Oh, yeah, my parents like all this shit." He motioned to the clean, fancy decor. "Here, my room's this way." He started down the stairs to the basement. I followed him, and once we entered, it all made a little more sense. His room was messy, with blankets and clothes strewn about the floor, and classic rock and psychedelic posters taped over every inch of the walls. A lava lamp sat on his desk which also held a laptop computer and some sheet music.

"This looks more like you," I said, as my skin crawled with anticipation. I didn't know where to sit, how to stand, what to say. I put my hand on my hip and then quickly back down to my side as I tried to appear relaxed.

"Andrea..." He was calm as he sat on the edge of his bed, the blue flannel sheets stretching beneath him. "Come here." He patted the spot next to him.

I thought about how pissed my mom would be if she knew I was alone in a boy's room without any parents home. But God it felt good to be there. And I appreciated that Josh was so collected. At least he could guide me through this unknown territory.

"Just relax," he said, as I awkwardly sat down, feet planted firmly on the floor and my back extended straight. "You know you're beautiful, right?" His voice got softer as he placed his hand gently on my face, brushing away a wisp of hair. His fingers felt electric against my skin, and I could feel the blood rushing through my body as I let out a nervous laugh. I couldn't bring myself to look in his eyes, because I knew he was going to kiss me if I did. I thought about Harper, how hurt she'd be if she knew what I was doing. How hurt I would be if the roles were reversed. But then my eyes lifted and met his gaze, and it was too late. His soulful brown eyes swallowed me up, and I wasn't thinking about Harper anymore.

He slowly leaned in, and I closed my eyes. I felt his bottom lip graze mine and he smiled, breathing out a sexy little laugh of disbelief.

"Andrea Cavanaugh," he whispered as his hand met my jaw. "I can't believe I'm kissing you." I didn't speak. Or move. But I surprised myself with my sudden boost of confidence as I nestled my hand behind his head and felt his messy hair between my fingertips.

He kissed me again, harder this time, and cradled my face while he maneuvered around my begging mouth. After a few moments, we finally paused, and I moved my head back, resting our foreheads together and breathed him in. He was musky, smoky, and I was surprised how much I liked it.

"You know what you're doing," I offered.

Josh's lips curled into a sweet smile as he looked down. "I've wanted to do that since I met you. You're gorgeous."

No boy had ever called me pretty before, let alone gorgeous. I hated the way I looked. I was too tall, my hips were too wide, and my hair was too flat. But I felt like he saw something special in me. "Your full lips, your big doe eyes … you're stunning."

"Stop," I whispered, though inside I was desperate for him to continue.

He kissed me again, softer this time, and eventually did show me that Pavement album, which of course I loved. And when we went upstairs, he sat down behind the baby grand piano in that expensive living room and started playing. It was a song I'd never heard before, but I didn't care. It was beautiful. He was beautiful. There was no seat near the piano, so I sat on the floor, feeling the plush white carpet under my hands, and listened, praising him as he paused. I was mesmerized.

"Shit," I said when I looked at my phone. It was 5:30 PM. My parents would be home soon. "I've gotta go."

"Aww, already?" He stood up from the piano bench.

I got up, too, and headed towards the door. "Thanks for today. I guess I'll see you tomorrow," I replied, unsure of what to say, unsure of what this meant. Josh extended his arms and nodded in my direction, signaling me to come over. I stepped closer, and he wrapped his arm around my waist and drew me in for a final kiss. I pressed into him as he moved his lips to my cheek, my jaw. Steadying my stance, I backed away. "Talk soon?" I opened the door.

He winked. "Bye, beautiful," he said softly.

As I heard the door close behind me, I took in a deep breath. I wanted to remember the way I felt right then, looking out at the golf course, having just been fawned over by someone so exotic and alluring. I felt insatiable, invincible. And I had to tell somebody.

Oh no, I said to myself as I remembered. *Harper ... ugh...*

Would she understand? Should I even tell her?

Maybe this was a one-time thing, and she'd never have to know. But I didn't want it to be a one-time thing. I drove home quickly as my mind raced. Then I remembered Stephanie. She would know what to do.

Chapter Five

Stephanie Lang was my childhood best friend. After Harper and I had become close last year, I stopped seeing Stephanie as often. She didn't seem to mind. She was developing her group of friends within the choir and drama circle, which didn't always mix well with the band squad. But we stayed in touch regardless. Our history was special to each of us, and we shared a lot of important coming-of-age memories. Plus, she was someone I trusted, someone who knew me better than almost anyone. She'd be the perfect sounding board for this Josh/Harper situation.

When I pulled in, I noticed my mom's car wasn't in the driveway yet, so I raced up to my room and dialed Stephanie's cell.

"Well Andrea Cavanaugh, as I live and breathe. What up, girl!" she exclaimed through the phone. Always outgoing, Stephanie's familiar friendly energy instantly made me feel at ease.

"Steph, I need some advice. I think I did something wrong."

"*No* way, not you. What'd you do, get a B+ on your report card?"

I loved Stephanie, but she always knew how to make me feel young and inexperienced. Contrary to what my faded siren-red highlights and vintage punk rock t-shirts might have one believe, I was referred to as the "goody goody" amongst our friends. I never missed curfew, I made good grades, had big dreams of a fancy college degrees, and was admittedly a little pretentious about how straight edge I was. I just never saw the appeal of the party scene. My parents drank almost every night and it never looked fun. It was mind-numbingly annoying to watch them sloppily tell me they loved me in between giggles.

Regardless of my reasons, my lack of enthusiasm for alcohol and pot didn't win me a lot of popularity points, so I tried to go the opposite direction with my appearance. It kept people on their toes, I think. It gave me the edge and friends I wanted without having to actually do anything I opposed or was too scared to try. But Stephanie always had a subtle (and sometimes not so subtle) way of reminding me about this.

"Did you not finish your vegetables? Or, gasp, God forbid, forget to make your bed this morning? Mrs. C must be *so* mad," Stephanie teased.

"Ha ha, Steph, I get it. No really, I need your help." I found myself excited to tell the story. After all the grown-up scenarios I'd been there for Stephanie for, from pregnancy scares to covering for her when she drank too much with her college-aged boyfriend, it was finally my turn to have something slightly salacious to share.

"So you know Josh McMillan?" I asked.

"Oh yeah, new kid, the piano prodigy, kinda weird? Oh wait, isn't he the one that you and Harper Cooley are always drooling over?"

"Stephanie! Is it that obvious?" I sighed while she laughed. "Whatever, yes, that's him. Anyway..."

"Oh shit, Andie, what did you do?"

I told her the whole story—the kissing, the guilt, and my confusion as to where to go from here.

"Wow, girl. I gotta say, I'm kinda proud. So you have to tell Harper, obviously."

"No..." I groaned. "Really? Ugh."

"Yes, dummy. Tell Harper what happened, that *Josh* instigated it, and ask her how she feels. If she's hurt, then you can't see him again. Sisters..."

"I know, I know, sisters before misters," I cut her off. "But he's so..."

"Nah nah nah, I don't care. If Harper's a good friend, she'll be happy for you. Maybe you'll be surprised. But I thought you were jonesing for Carter Wells? When did that change?"

"Um, maybe when I realized that no human specimen as ridiculously perfect as Carter Wells would ever consider going out with me? Or maybe when Carter started dating that skinny college girl who hangs out with Kid A? Or maybe when I remembered that every girl who's ever met Carter Wells has a crush on Carter Wells? I don't know, Steph, maybe one of those times?"

"Geeze, okay. I get it. Sorry, Debbie Downer. I just thought you liked him. And then suddenly this Josh swoops in out of nowhere."

"Look, Carter is a pipe dream, a fantasy. Josh is real, like this could actually happen for me. But you're right, I will talk to Harper."

"Good. Let me know how it goes. I got to run. I'm meeting Nick for dinner in a few. But you got this, okay? You little vixen."

"Very funny. Okay, thanks, talk soon." I hung up and stared at my phone. "Text me..." I whispered to it as if it could hear me. I was dying to hear from Josh in hopes I could decipher any message he'd send me to figure out what he was thinking. Did he want to date me? How much did he like me? Did he see a future with me?

"Andrea!" I heard my mother call from downstairs as I heard the front door close.

"Up here, Mom!"

I knew Stephanie was right. I had to talk to Harper. But not tonight. Tomorrow was Friday, and we had plans for her to sleep over, so I'd do it then. That way I'd have another day at school and another round of band practice to analyze Josh's behavior.

****

The next day at school, I barely saw Josh. I had spent extra time getting ready that morning, too. I even felt mildly pretty for a change. *He* had wanted to kiss *me*. I couldn't stop thinking about it. I got nervous as the school day ended, knowing I'd see him at jazz band practice. So I walked to the band room, but before I reached the door, I felt a warm hand on my waist, and the breath left my body as I turned around to see Josh.

"Hey you," he whispered. "Can I see you this weekend?"

It wasn't a dream. It wasn't an accident. Josh liked me.

"Yeah, text me." I tried to play it much cooler than I was.

"Nice. See you soon, miss conductor." He playfully saluted me before jogging over to chat with Ethan by the drum set.

"Hey, Andie," Harper said from behind me.

I jumped. And felt my breath snap back into my body as I reentered reality. "Oh hey, Harper, what's up? Still coming over tonight?"

"Duh!" she replied.

The next few hours floated by. I was stuck between being confused and thrilled by the Josh situation and anxious and guilty about the Harper situation. By the time she came over that night, I was ready.

"Hey, Harper, before we head to the movie, I want to talk to you about something," I said.

"Uh oh," she replied. "You're making me nervous. What?"

I took a breath and blurted it out. "Josh likes me. I mean, I think Josh likes me. He kissed me. I didn't know what to do. Nothing else happened. This was just yesterday. I'm so, so sorry. I understand if you're mad."

"Whoa." She took a long pause that filled the room with apprehension. "Are you guys, like, dating?" she finally asked.

"No! No, I don't even know what this means, but regardless, I would never be with him, like officially, unless you were cool with it. And I don't even know if that's what he wants. I just, ugh, I'm sorry, I don't know, I just wanted to talk to you before anything else happened."

"Well ... do you like him? Like really like him?" Harper asked.

"I think I do. It feels special. But I won't see Josh again if you don't want me to."

"Don't be silly. Don't let me stand in the way. If you guys like each other, I'm happy for you. Go for it." She forced a smile. I knew she didn't mean it, but honestly, I didn't care. I had gotten the permission I had sought out to receive, so I wasn't about to ruin this for myself by going on and on.

"Oh my God, Harper, you are the best!" I threw my arms around her in a hug. "Thank you so much!"

"Yeah, yeah, it's all good." She was lying through her teeth. She wasn't okay with this. She was fuming, and I knew it. I knew it because I would've done the same thing. But she was gracious and polite, and I let the guilt slide right off of me as it quickly was replaced by my anticipation of a possible boyfriend.

"What about Carter?" Harper asked.

"Why does everyone keep saying that? I'm not blind. Carter Wells is never gonna happen. And even if he somehow didn't think I was a complete loser, we both know Kid A would never loosen their grip on him."

"Right, I guess."

I knew she was just trying to find plausible holes

in my Josh scenario. But there was nothing plausible about Carter. He was gorgeous. Not just gorgeous, but *effortlessly* gorgeous. He was tall, slender but strong, with big mysterious eyes, shoulder-length dark wavy hair, and perfectly chiseled cheekbones that deserved their own fan club. And he was cool. He sang in a local rock band, studied art at the community college, and had a loft above his dad's garage where his bandmates and the other equally cool older kids hung out on the weekends. But he was so much different than everyone else. Carter was genuine, and kind, and every version of his smile was sexier than the last. I rarely saw him, except when I would tag along with Ethan, who was friends with Carter's drummer, to their local concerts. Sometimes we'd stick around after their shows and hang out, but I was always intimidated and had a hard time forming words when Carter would speak to me.

It was no secret that I had been crushing on Carter Wells for years, but the more I learned about him, the more I learned that it was no secret that *everybody* was crushing on Carter. He could've had his pick of any girl, and the fact that he had chosen Sloane Davison was not a surprise to anyone.

She was stunning. Her perfectly shaped eyes were outlined by Dior mascara and her petite, thin yet voluptuous figure was everybody's envy. She ran with Kid A when she was in high school, but she'd graduated last year and had enrolled at a nearby art school. And I hated it. But I knew Carter was way out of my league, so I tried to focus less and less on him over time, though I couldn't help but study every inch of him whenever we shared the same room. But now something real was happening for me. I wasn't just gazing and thinking. My attraction to Josh was being reciprocated, and it made the Carter pill a lot easier to swallow.

"Well let's head out. I don't want to miss the previews," Harper said.

"Oh, okay. You don't want to talk about this more?" I asked, surprised. I had assumed this conversation would be at least an hour of back-and-forth, and I'd prepared several talking points in my head that I was ready to pull out at a moment's notice.

"What else is there to talk about? It's all good, Andie. I'm happy for you." She was lying again. So I let her.

"Okay great. You are the best."

"Yeah yeah, you owe me." She laughed. "Let's go."

Chapter Six

Over the next couple of months, Josh and I settled into a nice routine. We spent most afternoons together after band practice, and most weekends together with Ethan, Harper, and sometimes others. When Josh asked me to be his girlfriend a couple of weeks into hanging out, I was overjoyed. Everything in my life felt different with a boyfriend. I started dividing my life into Josh moments and non-Josh moments.

We spent a lot of time kissing. I was starting to get used to it, and maybe even good at it. Ironically, we listened to the *Kid A* album during most of our make out sessions. It was unbelievably hot, and I would spare no detail when I boasted about it to Stephanie and Harper. Even Ethan said he'd never seen me so happy. I was different. Somebody liked me. Somebody *wanted* me, and it felt good.

Even though I was enjoying myself, I couldn't shake these odd intricacies that would pop up every once in a while. He was unapologetically hard on himself, especially when it came to the piano. He hated when I doted on how gifted he was, and he always turned the conversation into some kind of joke or funny banter, so eventually, I stopped complimenting his musical prowess altogether. I wanted him to feel like he could be comfortable with me, and I was careful not to push him anywhere he didn't want to go.

In my mind, he was a tortured, brilliant artist, and I could be the one who helped him, who figured him out. So it became my mission.

One Friday evening, Josh took me to Madres, my favorite Mexican restaurant, and we were talking and laughing as Josh made his best impression of Mr.

Thompson, our band teacher.

"And a one and a two … come on, kids, it's not rocket science!" Josh joked, heavily mocking Mr. Thompson's sharp Midwestern accent.

I was laughing so hard I had to catch my breath as our food came.

The server brought me a steaming plate of veggie enchiladas while he laid a plate of carne asada tacos in front of Josh.

I picked up my fork and dug in. "God, Josh, you nail that impression. It's too good." I took a bite.

Josh's eyes winced a bit.

I continued. "You have to show Ethan. It will slay him." I took another bite.

Josh winced again. "Hey, babe, do you think you could, ya know, oh never mind," he said.

"No, what?"

"It's nothing, forget it."

"Josh, you're making me paranoid. Please tell me."

"It's just ... when you eat, your fork hits your teeth loudly, and it's kinda annoying. Do you think you could, I don't know, eat a little bit quieter? Maybe just try not to use your teeth so much when you take a bite?"

I put my fork down and looked at him, searching for the humor in his eyes. "Ha ha, very funny." I smirked, assuming he was joking, but stopped quickly when his expression didn't change. He was serious.

"It's okay, Andie." He grabbed my hand. "It's just a little loud, but you can be quieter, right? It's all good, babe." His eyes looked earnest as he spoke. "Sorry, sweetie, I'm just a little particular about certain things. I hope you understand."

"Of course," I said slowly, though my mind went in a million directions. I felt a little uncomfortable, but mostly confused. I shrugged it off, reminding myself that everyone had their own idiosyncrasies, and this was just one of Josh's.

"That's my good girl." He started talking about the new piece our band was working on, but I had a hard time listening. I took a few more bites, surprised at how obsessed I became over each motion. Nobody from Kid A bit their fork that loudly, I bet. But I tried to shake off the thought, figuring I was making this a bigger deal than it was.

That night, I called Harper when I got home, dying to get another opinion on this bizarre moment.

"I don't know, Andie. It's kind of weird," she said after I gave her the story.

"Really? Ugh, I thought so too, but I don't know, maybe it's just one of his things."

"Yeah, maybe, but who even notices things like that? Maybe he's some weird OCD type?"

"He's not." I started to feel defensive. "I'm probably just overthinking this."

"Yeah maybe, but it *is* legit weird. You wanted a second opinion, so there you go."

My conversation with Harper didn't make me feel any better, but I tried to stop worrying about the strange incident. I had almost forgotten about it completely until that Monday at school when I met up with Josh and Harper for lunch. As we settled into a small table near a back corner of the cafeteria, Josh swung one arm around my shoulder and used the other arm to pick up his turkey sandwich. I always loved his public displays of affection. It was as if he wanted to remind the world that we were together.

Everything seemed normal as Josh bemoaned about his heavy homework load and I provided the occasional commentary from behind my small bag of potato chips. Harper started digging into her chop salad, and as she brought the plastic fork to her mouth, she chomped down loudly. And then, after she swallowed a mouthful of lettuce, she playfully started gnawing on the fork, to an exaggerated degree. You could probably hear her teeth against the plastic from several tables away. I cringed when I realized what she was doing, and Josh stopped mid-sentence when he figured it out, too.

When Harper realized she had gotten our attention, she burst into laughter. "You should see your faces!" she cackled. "Come on, Josh, it can't bother you *that* much. It's a fork for Christ's sake."

Josh slowly took his arm off my shoulder and stiffened his posture. There was a painful awkwardness in the air, but Harper didn't seem to notice.

"You're crazy," she teased, before changing the subject.

Josh was quiet for the rest of lunch. I could tell he was put off, but I figured he was just embarrassed. When lunch ended, and Harper headed to her calculus class, Josh grabbed my elbow and pulled me to the side of the main hallway, away from the traffic of students bustling by us.

"I can't believe you told her about that," he said sternly.

"I didn't think it was a big deal. As Harper said, it's just a fork, babe."

"It *is* a big deal to *me*. I thought you got that."

"Oh, I'm sorry. I didn't realize..."

"No. You didn't. What happens between us in private *stays* private. Okay?"

"Yeah, okay..." I trailed off. His eyes were cold and absent of their usual lively energy. I couldn't believe he was making such a big deal out of something so silly, but I wanted him to understand I valued his confidentiality and that it was safe to talk to me about anything. I wanted to be a good girlfriend, and it wasn't worth arguing about a fork. I could eat quieter if that's what he needed. I thought about the playlists, the cute text messages, and his affectionate behavior. And I reminded myself how lucky I was to be with such a sweet, vivacious guy. I could overlook something like this for the good of our relationship. So I told myself it would be all right, that everything would be okay. But it was never okay again.

Chapter Seven

The next day, Josh, Harper, and I decided to spend our lunch break at a sandwich shop near the school. As upperclassmen, we had off-campus privileges during lunch. When we got to the counter, I studied the chalkboard menu hanging above the cash register to try and find a side dish that didn't involve a fork. I didn't want to embarrass myself again, and I wasn't sure I'd yet mastered the quiet biting technique Josh had expected of me.

Mac and cheese? No. Coleslaw? Definitely not. A-ha! French fries. Perfect. After we ordered, we sat down and waited for our food.

"Whoa, check it out, it's Carter and Sloane," Harper said quietly, her eyes pointing toward the door. Josh and I both turned our heads to see our small town's version of the royal couple make their way to the front counter. Carter was breathtaking, per usual. It was almost as if I could see a literal glow around him as he stood there, pouring over the sandwich menu. He had this uncanny way to look grungy but not messy, sexy but approachable, creative but down-to-earth. Basically, he looked like what would happen if Zac Efron and Kurt Cobain reproduced to make one perfect, 19-year-old human. And then there was Sloane, hanging on Carter's arm, with a trendy leather headband atop her thick, wavy hair, and a fringed crop top that showed off her perfect, toned stomach. God, I hated her.

"Uh ... so? Who's that?" Josh asked.

"Seriously?" Harper replied. "Carter Wells is the singer of Intentionally Blank."

"Oh, yeah, I guess I've heard them," Josh said. "They're not that good."

"Yeah right," Harper scoffed. We both knew Josh was probably a little jealous that he wasn't the only musical prodigy in the room. I tried to change the subject to make him less uncomfortable, but it quickly broke when Carter approached our table.

"Hey, Andrea. Hey Harper, how you guys doing?" Carter asked politely.

Sloane was sitting at their table across the restaurant, intensely concentrating on her phone.

"Hi," I said shyly. The air felt better with Carter in it. My heartbeat quickened as he stood next to me.

"Hey, man, I don't think we've met," Carter said to Josh, reaching his hand out which Josh met with a weak shake.

"Yeah, Josh McMillan," he grumbled.

"*Oh* right, I've heard of you, the piano genius, right?"

Josh immediately perked up.

"Yeah, and Josh is Andrea's boyfriend," Harper awkwardly pointed out, even though nobody had asked. I think she wanted to make it clear that I was taken and she was not, though it was a moot point as Carter's pretty, petite girlfriend waited for him in the booth nearby.

"All right then," Carter said smiling. "Well, nice to see you guys. Have a good lunch."

Ugh, I thought to myself. *That could've gone better*. Even though I knew Carter was merely a fantasy, part of that stupid fantasy was hoping that he thought about me sometimes, and embarrassing run-ins like this didn't help that feel like much of a reality.

Harper and Josh started talking, and I tried to pay attention but kept catching myself stealing glimpses of Carter across the room. Even just looking at him was thrilling.

At one point near the end of our meal, Josh got up

to refill his clear, plastic water cup, but instead of selecting water at the fountain machine, he picked Coca-Cola. As the soda fizzed into his cup, the woman behind the cash register yelled from the counter.

"Hey! You didn't pay for that. If you ask for a cup for water, please only fill it with water," she shouted. "Goddamn kids," she mumbled under her breath. I saw Carter and Sloane give each other a knowing eye roll and share a quiet laugh. I was mortified at the idea of Carter Wells thinking that, through association, I was just lumped into the "bratty teenager" demographic.

"Of course, no problem," Josh said in an eerily cheery voice as he poured out his drink and quickly replaced it with water. Every part of me wanted to cringe with humiliation as I watched Josh saunter back to our table.

"Haha, nice try," Harper laughed. But I didn't think it was funny.

As we left the restaurant, I looked down at the dirty tile floor, hoping not to make eye contact with Carter or Sloane, but I couldn't help but look up to catch one last glimpse. Carter caught my eye and gave me his signature half smile as I walked through the door. My knees felt a little weak in the parking lot, but I tried to shake it off by the time we got to the car. That, back there, that was a dream life. This here, in this little white hatchback car, this was real. And I had to be okay with that. At least I had a boyfriend.

Chapter Eight

As my relationship with Josh progressed, Harper was surprisingly cool about it. The three of us spent a lot of time together that winter, Harper and Josh sometimes getting lost in conspiracy theories and references to classic rock bands I'd never heard of. I tried to keep up but was clearly out of my element when they'd go off on their tangents. Josh would dive into these conversations with his arm securely wrapped around me while he spoke, so I would tune out and just nestle into him while they talked. I loved feeling close to him, so I didn't care if they talked all night, as long as his arm stayed around me.

One night, we had parked in a local field, the three of us leaning on the hood of Harper's car while we talked about our futures, our breath visible in the freezing air. Harper couldn't wait to start college next year. We were both jealous, but I found myself feeling a little happy that I'd have Josh more to myself when Harper went away. I checked my phone and saw it was getting close to curfew.

"We'd better get going," I said, pointing to the time.

"Aw come on, Andrea," Josh pleaded. "Aren't your parents out tonight anyway? Let's stay out. I think Nicole is having people over. I can text her."

Nicole? The leader of Kid A? I silently asked myself. Since when was Josh talking to her?

"Oh?" I commented, trying not to sound panicked.

"Yeah!" Harper responded. "I'm in!"

Harper hated Nicole, even more than I did. This didn't feel right. But I knew I wasn't going to miss my curfew. I knew it was uncool, but I never considered disobeying my parents' lenient requests. I loved them, and they were always supportive of me. They even looked the other way when I showed up to church two years ago with bright pink hair. Maybe it was some silent understanding we had—they drank, I dyed my hair and sewed punk rock patches on my skirts, and it somehow evened out. I knew if I rocked the boat now, they would have a reason to be strict, which was the last thing I wanted, especially with just another year and a half before I moved away for college.

"No, guys," I protested. "I can't." I assumed that would be the end of it.

"Okay, we'll drop you off on the way," Josh said.

I was furious, but couldn't let them know. I needed Josh to think he was dating a chill girl who didn't let these things bother her. I shot a desperate glance to Harper, who just shrugged and looked down. *Bitch*, I thought. But then I remembered that I wasn't exactly in a place to be asking anything of Harper after what I pulled by dating Josh in the first place, so I just nodded as my blood boiled.

When they pulled up to my house, Josh didn't even kiss me goodbye.

"Peace out, babe, I'll call you tomorrow," he said, as Harper backed out of my driveway.

I was dumbfounded but tried to collect my thoughts.

He's allowed to have friends, I told myself. *Just chill out.* I went inside and flopped down on the plush blue sectional in the living room. I pulled my phone out of my purse, hoping they'd text me and apologize. I bit my nails as I waited, opening my Instagram app and scrolling through my feed to kill time. The first picture I saw was Carter and Sloane, taking a selfie from the front row at some concert, her stupid pretty face pressed against his. They looked happy, which put me in an even worse mood. How did they do it? How could they be so cool without trying? I spent every second of every day double checking and second guessing my every move, and even that wasn't good enough. I was still the girl who bit my fork too loudly and went home instead of to a party with my boyfriend. Carter just *was* cool. He didn't have to try. I felt enamored by that mystery. I scrolled down and saw Ethan pop up in my feed next. He was at Nicole's party with his Kid A girlfriend. *Traitor*! I thought, before remembering he didn't even know about my annoying evening.

I typed a text to Ethan, already knowing the answer.

Me: What r u up to?

Ethan: Not much, just chillin w/ some of Kara's friends. U?

Me: Just got home. Bored.

Ethan: Whoa, Josh and Harper just showed up. WHERE U?

Me: Yeah. I know. Not loving tonight.

Ethan: Damn. Catfight! Rawr."

Me: Whatever.

Annoyed, I tried thumbing through a magazine but eventually just decided to go to bed.

The next morning, I woke up earlier than I meant to and walked downstairs after wrapping myself in an oversized bathrobe.

"Good morning, sweetheart," my mom said in a sing-song voice coming from the kitchen.

"Hi, Mom," I replied.

"Can I get you something? We have orange juice."

"No." I pulled a Diet Coke out of the fridge.

"Oh, Andrea, a little early for that, no?"

"I don't care." I opened the can. I knew I was being rude and I started to feel bad. "Sorry, just early."

"Yes, up before 10 AM on a Saturday, we're all very impressed," she joked. "What'd you get up to last night?"

"Hung out with Josh and Harper."

"You don't mind that Harper hangs around with you guys so much?"

"Mom! She's my best friend."

"I know, it's just ... a little odd, that's all. But whatever's clever!" she responded. "Hey, how's your friend, Stephanie Lang? I haven't heard you talk about her in a while."

"Oh. Good, I guess." I realized I hadn't seen Stephanie much lately. I guess I'd been spending a lot of time with Josh and Harper. "I should call her."

"Yes, I always liked her. Her mother is a doll."

"Yeah, we know."

"So, you and Josh ... getting pretty serious, huh?" Mom asked as she gripped a hot mug of coffee, likely covering up the fact that she was nursing a hangover from the charity event she attended the night before.

"Yeah, I guess." I shrugged, not wanting to give too many details.

"Why don't you invite him over tonight? Your dad and I would love to meet him officially. We can order pizza, and you guys can hang out here."

"Hmm, yeah okay." Inviting him to meet my parents might actually be a good way to remind Josh that we were moving in a serious direction. Plus, I wanted to see how he acted after last night. I texted him right away.

Me: Want to come over tonight? My parents want to meet u. I know it's lame but could be fun, we can chill in the basement afterward.

I assumed he knew this was code for the promise of a long make out session.

"What're you doing?" my mom asked as I stared at my phone.

"Waiting for him to respond."

"Well, hon, a watched pot never boils. Why don't you put your phone down? It's still early. He's probably not up yet."

"No, Mom, Josh hates when I don't respond quickly. I don't want to miss it when he texts back."

"Ok ... it's not that big of a deal, Andie. Why don't you go get dressed, and I'll make you breakfast?"

"Yeah, okay," I replied hesitantly, heading upstairs, my phone clutched in my hand.

Fifteen minutes later, my mom entered my room to find me sitting on my bed, still wrapped in the same bathrobe, staring at my phone. When she walked in, I looked up quickly and got on my feet.

"Andrea, don't tell me you've been sitting there looking at your phone this whole time. Get in the shower!"

"Fine, sorry!" I rushed into the bathroom, hurriedly undressing as I started the water. I tried to be quick, praying he wouldn't write back while I was in the shower. I knew he'd be upset if I was lazy in my response, and I hated upsetting him.

As I rinsed my hair, I heard a familiar ding as my phone lit up by the sink.

"Shit!" I said as I picked up the speed.

Ding.

I rinsed the soap from my body and stepped onto the bathmat.

Ding. Ding.

I grabbed a towel and ran it through my hair.

Di-ding. I scooped up my phone with wet hands,

dripping water on the screen.

Six texts from Josh. I opened the first one.

Josh: Cool. What time?

I smiled as I thought about Josh meeting my family and therefore further officializing our relationship, which, I thought, would leave less room open for paranoia and interpretation.

My gaze lowered to the second message.

Josh: U there?

Josh: Andrea?

Josh: Where R U?

Josh: WTF.

Josh: Oh, so you're ignoring me now?

I knew this would happen. I dried my hands off and started typing furiously.

Me: Sorry, babe, was in the shower. 6 PM tonight?

Josh: Long shower. Ok.

Why did I always pick the wrong time to do things? I tried to shake off the bad feeling and focus on my excitement for the upcoming evening instead.

*****

It was a little after 6 PM when Josh arrived. My dad opened the door.

"Well, you must be Josh," he bellowed, extending his hand for a shake.

"Uh, yeah. Jim, right?" Josh said, offering a limp hand to shake.

"Um, right. Jim. Or Mr. Cavanaugh is fine, too..."

"Dad!" I yelled as I ran toward the front door. "Hi, Josh, come in! Don't mind my dad. He won't bite."

"Hi, Josh," my mom said as he entered the kitchen. "It's nice to meet you officially. I saw you play when you guys performed last month. You know your way around a piano!"

"Yeah," he said quietly. I didn't know why he was being awkward. He was normally so fun and friendly. I didn't know why he couldn't show that side to my parents.

"So what do you like on your pizza? Jim was just about to order," my mom said, waving toward my dad.

"Oh, whatever," Josh replied. "I don't care."

"Okay then, Jim, get one veggie and one pepperoni."

"I'm on it!" my dad replied as he grabbed his phone.

"So, Josh, tell me about yourself. I've heard lots of good things." God bless my mother, she was a great talker. If anyone could make an awkward situation more comfortable, she could.

"I don't know," Josh said. After he had paused long enough for us to realize he wasn't going to give any more information, my mom jumped to the rescue.

"Moving to a new school in your junior year, that must've been tough, huh?"

"I guess."

"What about your parents? What do they do?"

"They're in banking."

"Well, that must be interesting."

"Not really."

My dad hung up the phone.

"Pizza is on the way!" he exclaimed, sitting on a stool at the kitchen counter. Another long, painful pause followed. I couldn't understand why Josh was making this so difficult. I wanted them to see the Josh I saw, so I tried rescuing the evening.

"Josh won the Mozart Award at his last school, the youngest person at the school to ever win!" I proudly boasted. Josh shot a look at me that made me instantly uncomfortable. Did I get a detail wrong? Was I not supposed to share that? His eyes tightened, and he glared at me, pursing his lips.

"Wow, that's something," my dad said.

"It's not a big deal," Josh said. "I thought I told Andrea that it wasn't a big deal, but she can't seem to get that through her head." Each word came out slowly and methodically.

I was trying to help, and I'd just made things worse. *Had* he told me that before? I couldn't remember. Had he asked me not to tell that story? I didn't recall, but he probably had, and I just didn't remember.

"Sorry," I murmured.

"No, I think that's great," my mom said. "That sounds like a very impressive award."

"It's not. That school was lame," Josh replied.

"Oh okay," my mom said, looking to my dad for help. Even she was having trouble navigating this conversation. My parents poured themselves each a large glass of wine, and my mom started talking about a friend of theirs who was traveling to Europe soon. She went into detail of every stop their friend planned to make, just trying to fill the air with something other than silence. Neither Josh nor I were listening at that point. We just let them talk and sip their chardonnay so they could feel comfortable. I nodded every once in a while to feign interest, but Josh didn't even try. He was just looking down, typing on his phone. I tried to cautiously look at what he was so focused on, but he was tilting the screen away from my glance.

"Josh, did you hear me?" my dad asked. "I said the pizza is here. Do you want to help me get it?"

"Oh. Uh, okay," Josh replied, setting his phone on the kitchen table as he got up to join my dad by the front door. When they were out of sight, I quickly darted my eyes toward his phone and saw Harper's name. My heart sank. Then I read his text.

Josh: This sucks. Meet me after?

I choked on my breath.

"Dinner's ready, ladies!" my dad said as he and Josh appeared back in the kitchen holding two pizzas.

Josh immediately scooped up his phone and shoved it in his pocket, unaware that I had seen it.

I told myself that I could fix this. I knew I had messed up the evening so far. I should never have asked Josh to do something so boring like meet my parents. I needed to keep his attention. I needed to remind him that I was his cool, fun girlfriend, that I wouldn't keep messing things up.

"Hey, Josh and I are going to take our pizza downstairs, okay?" I said to my parents, throwing a couple of slices on a plate and grabbing Josh's hand.

"Oh. Ok, sweetie. Josh, it was a pleasure meeting you," my mom replied.

"Yeah. Okay," Josh responded as I yanked him toward the basement stairs, closing the door behind us. We sat on the couch, and I shoved the plate onto the coffee table. I wasn't hungry anymore, I was on a mission.

"Andie, I'm probably gonna take off soon."

"How was Nicole's last night?" I asked, ignoring his statement, hoping to get his mind off of leaving.

"Great. Until I talked to Ethan."

"Why? What did he say?"

"He mentioned that you texted him that night. What the fuck, Andrea? You know you're *my* girl, right? Why are you texting Ethan late at night?"

I perked up. I was "his girl." I loved the way it sounded, and I loved his fierce protection of me.

"Ethan's my friend. You know that."

"Well, it's not cool. It makes me look bad, having

my girlfriend texting other guys all night. You don't want to make me look stupid, do you?"

"No of course not!"

"Then cut that shit out, okay?"

"Yes, okay. I'm sorry, babe."

"Good girl," he said softly. "Now come here. You look hot in that dress." He pulled me close to him and started kissing me. I felt instant relief. He still wanted me. I just had to stop messing up, but it was hard to know what was going to upset him, so I needed to do a better job of figuring it out ahead of time.

He kissed me hard, harder than normal. His lips felt rough, chapped. I pulled away a little bit, and he just tightened his grip around my waist. He started unbuttoning the front of my denim dress, breathing heavily as he fumbled.

"Whoa, Josh, hang on," I said.

He let go and pushed me away, shaking his head.

"I knew it. I knew you'd back out."

"I'm sorry," I said quietly, my face flushing. We had never gone farther than making out, and I could sense a building frustration about that from Josh. I didn't want to upset him, but I wasn't ready. I didn't feel willing to share that part of me with him yet, with anyone. I took a deep breath. Maybe I just needed to grow up. I wasn't ready to stop feeling wanted, desired. I knew how lucky I was to have Josh. Who knew how long it would be until someone else showed interest. What if it never happened? I couldn't let this end just because of some stupid rules I had made for myself. I needed to adapt. I was almost seventeen and the only one I knew who hadn't made it past first base.

"Never mind, I'll just get going," Josh said as he went to stand up.

"No, stop." I placed my hand on his leg. "Stay." I

started unbuttoning my dress, slowly at first, until my white bra started peeking out.

"Good girl," he whispered, sliding closer to me. He kissed my neck and crept his hand behind the fabric of my new dress as he caressed me through my bra. It was surreal, that moment. I didn't know what it would feel like, but I didn't think it would feel like this. I felt my body stiffen and I didn't know what to do with my hands, so I just rest them straight at my sides.

Just as I was starting to get used to the feeling and warm up to the idea, he pulled his hand off my breast and moved it to my thigh. I flinched, uncomfortable with where things were headed. He slid his hand up my leg until his finger was tracing the edge of my cotton panties.

"What're you do—" I tried to ask.

"That's my girl." He cut me off. "That's my girl. You're so beautiful."

I didn't have time to think. I barely had time to recognize what was happening when he pulled my panties aside and plunged a finger inside of me.

"Ouch!" I shouted, more out of shock than actual pain.

"Shh, baby." He motioned to the ceiling, a reminder that my parents were right upstairs. "You're doing so good."

If I made him stop now, I knew he would leave. And then he'd meet up with Harper and probably tell her, and everyone, what a prude I was. This was still little league stuff compared to what Stephanie and my other friends did. I was angry at myself for letting it bother me so much. I bit my lip and tried to relax, but it didn't feel good. His hands were rough and his motions jerky.

I didn't understand why people liked this. I loved making out. There was something sensual and alluring about that, but there was nothing special about this. Was

I supposed to say something? Tell him to stop? Tell him to keep going? Unsure and unwilling to say the wrong thing at such a vulnerable moment, I stayed quiet. He stopped kissing me at that point and rested his head on my shoulder while he continued touching me.

When he was finally tired, he pulled his hand away and smoothed out the skirt of my dress. He kissed my forehead and started buttoning my dress.

"Damn that was fun," he said, seemingly proud of himself. I meekly smiled and tried to nestle my head on his chest. He put his arm around me and sighed. I closed my eyes and took in the moment. This was all I wanted. To be held.

We turned on the TV and flipped through a few channels before we heard the basement door open. My mom came halfway down the stairs.

"It's getting late, Josh, probably time to head home."

"Cool," he replied. "Call you tomorrow, Andie." He winked at me. The sparkle had returned to his eyes. "Thanks for dinner, Mrs. Cavanaugh."

After Josh had left that night, my parents called me into the kitchen.

"So Josh is an interesting character," my mom started.

"He was a little off tonight," I said. "He's not normally so moody."

"Not the best first impression," my dad agreed. "What do you like about him, Andrea?"

"He's different. He's not like you and me, he thinks differently. And he's so talented. He's practically a genius. And he really likes me."

"Okay, just be careful, hon. We're not sure about Josh." My mom sounded worried.

"You just don't know him. It was a bad night. If

you had seen him any other time, you would've loved him. You don't see what he's like when we're alone. He's really sweet."

"Okay," my dad said. "Just make sure you take it easy, all right?"

"Yeah, don't worry guys. You'll see him another time, and it'll be better," I assured them.

When I crawled into bed that night, I couldn't fall asleep. I thought the first time I went this far with a guy, I'd be excited, dying to call Stephanie and prove I wasn't such a baby. But I didn't want to tell anyone. I felt different now, like I had crossed a line that I couldn't take back. But I told myself this was all part of growing up, and I had to get used to it. At least I had gotten him to stay. There was some power in that, I thought. And that, at least, was something to feel good about.

Chapter Nine

The next day at school, I met Josh by the band room at 7:15 AM sharp, our daily ritual.

"Hey, you." He greeted me warmly, in a seemingly good mood.

Phew, I thought. *It will be a good day.* I released the breath I didn't even realize I was holding.

"Guess what?" he asked, his smile gleaming, his energy contagious.

"What?" I returned his enthusiasm.

"You know how Seth and his friends were at our band performance last week?"

"Yes," I responded, remembering that Seth was Josh's friend from his last high school downtown. He was someone Josh spoke of often and seemed to admire. I only knew him from the occasional Instagram post.

"Well, I was texting with him last night. He knows about you and me, and he said that when he was watching you at the performance, you looked much skinnier in person than you did on Instagram. He thinks you're hot. I gotta say, I was pretty proud of you and that flat stomach." He patted my midsection with an open palm, which instantly caused me to tense up. "Whoa, babe, can't a guy touch his girlfriend? Jesus."

My mind was racing. *Much skinnier in person*, I kept thinking. That's a compliment, right? He was happy, right? Or was he implying I should change my Instagram photos? God, what photos was he talking about? How hideous did I look? He planted his hand on my stomach, more firmly now. I felt my body flex, but I forced myself not to flinch this time. He crept his finger under the hem of my shirt. His touch felt abrasive on my soft skin.

"I gotta jet, but I'll see *you* later, sexy." He turned

to go and stopped himself, whipping his head back. "Speaking of sexy ... Seth and I were talking, would it kill you to dress the part a little more?"

"Oh, um, okay," I said, unsure of what to think, how to move.

"Good girl," he said with a wink. I stood there motionless, not sure what to make of this conversation. Placing my hands on my hips, I pinched the excess skin that hung from my bone and hated every spec of it. It was soft and mushy and ugly. I suddenly hated my clothes, too. My jeans were too baggy, my flannel shirt was too old, my roots hadn't been dyed in months and probably looked ridiculous. I put my hand through my hair and despised how thin it felt. How did I expect someone like Josh to want to be with me? To be proud to hold hands with me at school? He was right. I had a lot of changes to make. But I would do it.

I thought this would be a good day, and here I ruined it before first period even started. But this time, I didn't mess things up by saying or doing something stupid like I usually did, I just ... was.

Before I could collect my thoughts any further, Ethan strolled through the band room door, slapping the door frame in a funky rhythm as he entered.

"What's up!" he announced, instantly noticing the disappointed look on my face. "Oh, I mean, what's up?" he said again, sounding concerned this time.

I shook my head quickly as if I could shake off the ugliness and reset.

"Nothing. Hi," I said.

"Thought I'd hear back from you last night. I wanted to see what you were up to."

"Oh. Right. Sorry. I had plans with Josh." I responded. *Shit. Josh.* I remembered how he'd asked me to steer clear of Ethan, how it made him look bad. As I saw other students passing the classroom door, I felt a panic start building inside me. What if someone saw us together and told Josh? What if he found out I was in here talking to Ethan alone? He'd be furious.

"I gotta go, Ethan, I'll see you around." I pushed past him as I walked quickly to the door.

"Uh ... okay ... are we, um, cool?" he asked.

I turned around and saw his eyes squint and head tilt as he inquired. Guilt started creeping in, but I pushed it aside and swallowed it down. My relationship had to be my first priority if I didn't want to lose the only guy who might ever care about me.

"It's fine, I just have to go," I said as I left the room.

The day went by slowly, and I couldn't concentrate on anything other than getting home and updating my Instagram photos. Luckily, there was no band practice today, so I'd have hours to myself after school. When the last bell rang, I made a beeline for my car and sped home. When I arrived, I walked up to the garage door and tapped in the code. As my fingers typed on the plastic keypad, I heard a motor with a familiar whir behind me and turned my head to see Josh's maroon sedan, pulling in right behind me. I stood frozen, confused. We hadn't made plans. Had we? Was I losing my mind?

"What the fuck, Andrea?" he said sharply, slamming the car door behind him. "You don't say goodbye? You think you can just take off like that?"

"I'm sorry?" I wasn't sure what I was sorry about, I just knew I was. He looked angrier than I'd ever seen him before. The sparkle was gone from his eyes, replaced by a cold, distant glare. As he walked toward me, I took a step backward. The closer he got, the deeper the pit in my stomach became. I'd seen him upset before, but this was different.

Without missing a beat, he extended his arm and gripped my jaw between his thumb and middle finger.

"I said, 'what the fuck,' are you deaf?" His voice rang out in a steady, distinct tone I would never forget. "I told some people we would meet up with them after school, and when I go to the band room to find you, I see you already in the parking lot. And I looked like an asshole when they asked if we were ready to go. And I'm driving behind you the whole way home, and you don't even notice? Are you an idiot?"

"B-but I *didn't* notice, Josh. I didn't see you," I managed to stammer from beneath his grip.

"Lying bitch." His eyes pierced me as he spoke, concentrating on each, angry word.

"Please, you're hurting me."

"Please, you're hurting me," he said back to me, mocking my voice. "God you really are an idiot."

I was in such disbelief. All I had wanted to do was show him what a good listener I was by hurrying home to fix my Instagram pictures. That way, he could feel better about showing me off to his friends. I wanted him to feel proud to have me as his girlfriend. But this was new, and unpredictable, and terrifying. And underneath my fear was a nagging voice telling me I had messed up again. Even when I was trying to do the right thing, I couldn't. Maybe it was time to stop trying. Maybe it was time just to exist. Or would I screw that up, too?

His hand tightened around my face, and I felt the tears forming behind my eyes. I felt like such a failure. I tried to speak but couldn't. He let go of his grasp in a quick, violent motion and brushed past me, letting himself into my house, leaving me paralyzed in the garage. I choked back a sob and steadied myself against the wall, rubbing my sore cheek. I had to fix this.

I opened the door slowly and stepped inside, seeing him sitting relaxed on the blue couch in my living room. I didn't know if I should go closer or farther, but I needed to stop guessing what he wanted because I was usually wrong. So I just stood there, awaiting further instruction.

"Come here. Sit down." I obeyed. "Were you crying?" he said, noting my red eyes and deep breaths. I didn't know what to say. If I said yes, would he show sympathy? Or would he just think I was being dramatic? So I looked at him, hoping my face would do the talking for me.

"Sweetheart, I'm so sorry, I don't like to make you cry," he said, wrapping his arm around me, pulling me into him. "You just have to understand where I'm coming from, right?" I nodded, swallowing hard. "You just make it tough sometimes, but you know I love you, right?"

My eyes widened. He loved me? He had never said that before.

"What? Is that a surprise?" he asked when I lifted my head, looking perplexed. "Of course I love you, Andrea. You're my girl." He kissed my forehead.

My face stopped hurting. I suddenly felt my body grow warm and excitement bubbled up into my chest, washing out the panic.

"I ... I love you too," I said, thinking that was the appropriate response. As I thought about it more that evening, I told myself that I did love him. He was fun and smart, and so talented. I knew he had an angry streak, but it wasn't anything we couldn't work through together, especially if we were in love.

After Josh left, I logged onto my computer and removed over 30 photos from Instagram that I deemed unflattering. In some of the pictures, my arms looked fat, in other pictures it was my legs, and there were a couple candid photos with bad lighting where my skin looked blotchy. Before I could replace them, I heard the garage door open. I closed my laptop and went down to the kitchen where I saw my mom setting down a bag of groceries.

"Hey sweetie," she said. "Sorry I'm late. I decided to stop at the store and get stuff so we could have taco night! We haven't done that in ages." She began unpacking.

"Thanks, but I'm not hungry." My stomach was still in knots from the day.

"Well, you have to eat. Come on, why don't you help me?"

"Ugh, fine," I groaned, secretly happy for the distraction. After my dad had arrived and we had dinner, I excused myself back to my room. I turned on my hair straightener and started applying mascara to get a good, new selfie. As I swept eyeshadow onto my lid, I started feeling uneasy, nauseous. I closed my eyes to take a deep breath, and I could hear Josh's voice. *Are you an idiot?* it sneered in my head. I felt his invisible hand around my face again and my stomach twisted. I ran to the bathroom and started heaving, only stopping to gasp for air. Each gasp was accompanied by a flashback to the garage, the fear creeping back into my body.

My mom swung the bathroom door open.

"Andrea!" she yelled, kneeling at my side. "What happened? Are you okay?" She pulled my hair back.

"I'm all right," I coughed. "I just don't feel good."

"I'm so sorry, honey. Come here, let's get you back to bed." She started running the water, wetting a washcloth. "Was it the food? Or are you just sick?"

"I don't know. I'm sorry."

"You have no reason to be sorry, Andie, just lay down. We'll see how you're doing in the morning. Just holler if you need anything, okay? I'll get you some water," she said as she walked out.

I felt like I was spinning. I tried to calm down my rushing body and took deep breaths.

He loves you, I told myself. *Somebody loves you*. I smiled, closing my eyes, feeling every inch of warmth that emotion brought with it.

My mom returned with a glass of water and turned off the lights.

I drifted to sleep without even washing off my freshly applied makeup.

The next day at school, I was a little nervous to face Josh. I wasn't sure which version of him I'd be met with today. Would it be the one who said he loved me? Or the one who grabbed my face and scolded me? I hoped the latter was just a fluke, perhaps sparked by a bad mood or a rough day. And when I met him in the band room before first period, I was relieved to see a smiling Josh as he outstretched his arms to give me a warm greeting.

"Hey, you," he said as he embraced me. "I feel bad about how things went down yesterday, so I got you a little something." I relaxed into him as I let out a breath, feeling reassured that the right Josh had shown up today. I was grateful for his apology. I knew he couldn't have meant those cruel things he said the day before. That wasn't the guy I knew. And while his sudden, unpredictable rage had really scared me, I hoped that it was behind us now, and we could just move forward with our newly professed love.

As Josh pulled back from our hug, he reached into his backpack that was sitting on a chair next to him. He pulled out some lavender cotton fabric and held it up for me to see. It was a t-shirt with my favorite band's logo stretched across the front.

"Oh my God! You're so sweet!" I reached for the shirt excitedly. "How'd you know Jack's Mannequin was my favorite?"

"I'd like to think I know you pretty well." He smiled. "So you like it?"

"I love it! Thank you so much!" I held it up to my chest and paused when I noticed the width was much narrower than I had expected. My waist was significantly wider than the fabric offered, so I checked the tag and saw it was a size small.

"What's wrong, babe?"

"Oh, nothing, it's just ... I think it's a little small, that's all. But maybe I can exchange it?"

"Nah, it'll fit soon I'm sure. You were planning on losing a little weight anyway, right?"

My heart dropped. "Right," I said softly. I knew I wasn't the skinniest girl at the school, and I knew could probably stand to lose five or maybe even ten pounds, but I never realized it was so noticeable. I suddenly felt disgusting in my own skin.

"Just think of it as a goal or something. It'll look great on you!"

"Yeah, okay. Thanks." I didn't know what else to say. I stuffed the t-shirt into my backpack and tried to smile at Josh, so he didn't see how upset I was.

"So you like it? I was excited to get it for you. You know I love you, right?"

My smile widened when I heard those words, and I started to feel a little better. Maybe he was just trying to help me be the best version of myself. It *was* a cool shirt, and it was nice that he got me a gift, especially after yesterday. I probably just needed to relax a little bit.

"Me too. I mean, I love you too."

The bell rang.

He leaned in and kissed me quickly on the lips.

"See you later, beautiful."

As I walked to my first class, I kept pulling at the hem of the shirt I was wearing, feeling like I needed to stretch it out, so my figure was less noticeable. If Josh could tell I was overweight, it probably was no secret to the rest of the school, too.

I tried not to let it bother me, but throughout the day I kept shifting positions when I would sit or stand, trying to figure out the most flattering posture that hid as much of me as possible. Even if it wasn't real, I needed to give the illusion of someone thinner, prettier, better. I studied Nicole in the hallways and envied her confidence. But if my legs looked that good in a short skirt, I'd probably have her conviction, too.

I tried to hold my head high the rest of that day, but whenever I caught myself in a mirror or saw that lavender material peek out of my bag, I would think of my hips and be embarrassed all over again. I felt nauseous again that evening and skipped dinner, knowing I wouldn't be able to keep it down.

When I got into bed that night, the hunger started creeping in, but I didn't mind. It actually felt kind of powerful. The joy I got from thinking about how happy and aroused Josh would be to see me flaunting that small shirt one day overpowered the growling in my stomach, and I finally fell asleep, though the relief was short-lived.

I woke up with a sharp, sudden breath and felt a cold sweat dripping from my skin. The room was still dark except for the glow of the digital clock on my bedside table. It was a little after midnight and I was having trouble catching my breath. Did I have a bad dream? I couldn't remember, but suddenly wasn't able to get comfortable again. I placed my hand on my stomach when I felt the hunger pang come back but reminded myself to push through it. I decided to sneak downstairs for some water in hopes that would help.

As I got midway down the staircase, I heard faint sounds of laughter coming from the living room, and when I got closer I saw my dad stretched out on the couch in his blue silk pajamas and bathrobe, watching *The Tonight Show*. He muted the TV and sat up when he saw me.

"Andie? Everything okay?" he said, fumbling for his glasses on the armrest.

"Yeah, just can't sleep."

"Join the club." He smiled with tired eyes. "Come sit down. This guy's pretty funny." He motioned toward the TV screen.

"I've seen this show before. It's not *that* funny."

"When have you been up late enough to watch *The Tonight Show*? Ya know what, never mind." He chuckled. "Probably better I don't even know."

I shrugged and flopped down next to him, leaning my head against the back of the couch and tucking my knees to my chest. He tossed me a blanket and unmuted the show.

"So, I've got a big presentation at work tomorrow and can't stop going over it in my head. What's your excuse? Why aren't you sleeping?" he asked, keeping his eyes on the television.

I shrugged again. "I don't know, just can't."

"Everything okay? School okay?"

"Yeah. Dad, you don't have to do this."

"Do what? Talk to my daughter?"

"We can just watch the show, it's cool."

"Everything okay with Josh?"

"Dad! Yes! God."

"I'm just asking! I can't ask about your life?"

"Sorry. You can. I'm just tired. But everything's fine. Don't worry." I tried to smile.

"You know, when I was your age, I was in my first relationship, too. I like to think I had a pretty awesome girlfriend."

"Yeah yeah, we all know. Mom was the cutest girl at school. You had a cool car and cooler hair. I could probably tell this story in my sleep."

"You can't blame me for wanting to brag," he said with a dopey grin.

"High school sweethearts, young lovebirds, you guys are a walking cliché," I teased.

"But a cliché with a cool car and cooler hair, right?"

"Maybe once, Dad." I giggled.

He pretended to look offended but couldn't keep himself from laughing. I grabbed the remote and turned up the volume on the TV. The show was funnier than I remembered. After a few minutes, I heard a snore come from my dad's direction. I playfully hit him in the arm and he jolted up.

"Go to bed, Dad," I offered.

"Geeze, guess I dozed off. All right, I'm gonna head up. You coming, Andie?"

"Not yet," I said. "Is it okay if I stay here until I get tired?"

"Yeah, sure. See, I told you this was a good show! Just try and get to bed soon, okay?"

I nodded and watched my dad drift toward the stairs from the corner of my eye. The hunger pangs came back when he disappeared, and suddenly the room felt empty and small. I had the whole couch to myself but couldn't get comfortable stretching out, so tried to snuggle into a corner. Closing my eyes only made the empty nausea worse, so I turned off the TV and tried to find comfort in the still darkness, but there was no comfort there.

Chapter Ten

By the time the second semester rolled around, Josh and I had fallen into a more predictable routine, which I liked, but I had barely seen Ethan or Stephanie in months. Their lives seemed to continue without me as I watched through the hallways. Ethan and his Kid A girlfriend had broken up. I felt guilty I wasn't there for him, but now that he was single, I knew Josh would be even angrier if we spent time together, so I tried to back off as much as possible.

Harper was getting ready for college. That was all she talked about. "Next year when I'm at Michigan," was how practically every sentence started. She and I spent lunch every day with Josh and then would talk in the band room after school while Josh practiced the piano. He was preparing for the upcoming talent show in which he planned on playing and singing "Space Oddity" by David Bowie, a song that Harper suggested. They had been working on it together a lot after school. I didn't mind. I knew Harper was a huge Bowie fan, and Josh valued her feedback.

"Did you hear the news about Ethan?" Harper asked one day after school, while Josh practiced the piano behind us in the band room.

"No, what about him?" I hoped Josh overheard my question, so he knew I wasn't keeping up with Ethan.

"He's the new drummer for Carter Wells' band."

"*What*? No way!" I said. Intentionally Blank was the biggest local band around. Everyone went to their shows. I kept picturing Ethan hanging out in Carter's loft with all the guys from that band, especially Carter.

"Yeah, apparently Alex dropped out of the band to focus more on school or whatever. So Carter heard

Ethan was a sick drummer and invited him to try out. I think he's been playing with them a couple of weeks now. Their next show is in April. We should all go!" she said, motioning to Josh and me.

"Yeah maybe," I said. "It's up to Josh." He didn't respond. I wasn't sure if he was immersed in his music or just chose not to answer. I couldn't believe Ethan hadn't told me this. It was huge news. But I guess I hadn't been particularly approachable lately. There was that guilt creeping up again, but I swallowed it down and turned my attention to Josh.

"This sounds incredible, babe. You're going to kill it on Saturday."

"Ha, like you even know what Bowie is supposed to sound like," he retorted, sharing a smirk with Harper.

I looked down.

"Are you rehearsing tonight?" Harper asked him. "I can come by and give some final notes."

"Thanks but no thanks, Harp. I promised my girl Andie she could come over for a little romance. Right, babe?" I hadn't remembered making these plans but was happy he wanted to spend time with me.

"Right," I said.

After school, I met Josh at his house.

"Do you want to hear the whole thing from start to finish?" Josh asked, referring to the song he was preparing.

"Of course!" I took my usual seat on the white carpet next to his piano. He sat on the bench, looking down at me.

"Here it goes," he said. He began playing, and I was mesmerized by the melody. It was haunting, beautiful. And his voice filled the room in this big, exquisite way. I was so proud of him. I knew how hard he'd been working, and it sounded so, so good. As he got near the end, he drew his hands up and then just splashed them onto the keys, making a loud, crashing noise.

"What happened? You were doing great!" I said. He stood up so fast that the bench fell over behind him.

"It sucked! It fucking sucked. I couldn't even finish it. I can't play this on Saturday. I'm a fucking joke," he said, his voice elevating.

"Hey, Josh, no, it sounded fantastic," I reassured him as I stood up.

"How would you know?" His eyes turned cold. I felt the hair on my arms stand up and the increasingly familiar pit in my stomach returned.

"Honestly, you are so talented. It was great—" Before I could even finish, he struck my cheek with the back of his hand. I brought my hand to my face and stared at him, tears forming.

He grabbed my shoulders and shoved me into the wall of his living room, holding me there while he stared deep into my eyes, a hateful look on his face.

"You have no fucking idea," he harshly whispered. "Who the fuck do you think you are?"

He let go, and I sank down the wall, sitting back on the carpet. I hated that I was crying, but I couldn't stop. My face burned and my shoulders ached.

He turned and walked into the other room.

I sat there quietly while I heard him apparently on the phone.

"Harper? Yeah, it's me. Can you come over? I know I said I was busy, but I need you right now. I can't get the ending to sound good. Okay great, thanks, see you soon."

I took a few quick breaths, wiped my eyes with my sleeve, and got to my feet.

"Do you want me to go?" I asked quietly from the living room.

"Yeah, why don't you do that?" he snapped.

I slipped out the front door and got into my car. Alone now and with the immediate fear disappearing, my body let go, and I started sobbing. Not wanting to see Harper if she was on her way, I quickly started my car and drove off, parking at a nearby shopping center so I could collect myself before heading home.

What does this mean? Are we still together? Is it going to get worse? Is this the way all couples fight? My mind raced with questions as I picked up my phone and stared at it. I considered calling Stephanie or my mom but ultimately decided against it. They'd just tell me to break up with him without understanding what the consequences would be if I made him *really* angry. Plus, I didn't want them to look at Josh in only bad light. I knew they already weren't crazy about him, and this would be the final straw. Josh wasn't a bad guy. He just went through these angry episodes, and I knew nobody else could understand him as I did. I would just have to fix this myself.

When I got home that night, I couldn't eat again.

"I'm getting worried about your stomach," my mom said, sounding concerned. "You're either not eating, or you're throwing up what you eat. I'm scheduling a doctor's appointment for you."

"Okay," I muttered, not having the energy to argue about it. I went to bed early that night, turning the volume up loud on my phone so I would wake up if Josh tried to text me. Maybe he would try to apologize? But I slept all night, undisturbed.

****

When I saw Josh at school the next day, his good mood had returned.

"Hey you," he offered as if nothing had happened. "What's up?" he said, lightly kissing me on the same cheek he had struck the day before.

"Oh, um, nothing. Are you ... are you feeling better?"

"Better than what?" he said, tilting his head.

"Better than yesterday? Better about your song?"

His eyebrows turned down, and he looked perplexed, but before he could respond, Harper came bouncing toward us.

"Hey, guys! Oh my gosh Andrea you have to hear Josh's song. It's incredible," she gushed.

He smiled and looked down, lifting his gaze to look at Harper.

"I did hear it," I said. "Yesterday. I thought it was great."

Josh put his arm around my waist and started digging his fingers into my side, not visible to Harper but just enough to make sure I got the message. I did. We weren't supposed to talk about what happened yesterday. So I fell quiet as they talked, my head swimming. Harper's shrill laugh snapped my concentration, and I tried to focus on what they were saying.

"So tomorrow's the big day," Harper said, referring to the talent show.

"Yep, but I don't care. It'll just be fun to play," Josh replied.

I drifted through the rest of the day, speaking only when I was spoken to. It was easier that way. After third period, I saw Ethan at his locker. I knew Josh was in chemistry, on the other side of the school, so I decided to make contact quickly.

"Hi," I said, my eyes darting, searching for Kid A or other possible narcs. "Congratulations, I heard about Intentionally Blank."

"Oh hey. Yeah, thanks, it's been fun. You coming to our show?" Ethan asked.

"Maybe. It depends..."

He cut me off. "Depends on Josh ... figures. Sorry I asked."

"No, it's just..."

"Save it, Andrea. You've been completely MIA since you guys got serious, and I get it, I do, it's exciting, but I've been going through a lot, and you were nowhere to be found. Now suddenly you come say hi like nothing's up?"

"Ethan, I'm sorry," I said, realizing that word didn't even mean anything anymore. "I just wanted to say I'm happy for you. I get that this is a big deal."

"Yeah, you know what, it is. And Carter even asked me about you, asking if you'd want to come chill at the loft one day during practice. But I said you were too busy."

"Oh my God," I said, realizing Carter Wells not only didn't think I was a complete loser but actually thought about me enough to bring my name up in conversation. I wanted to shout that I *wasn't* busy, that I would be there anytime, but I knew I couldn't. If Josh was threatened by my friendship with Ethan, he would lose it if he knew I'd been hanging out with Carter. I bit my lip hard until it went numb.

"Yeah, well, I figure if you were too busy to talk after Kara broke up with me, you'd be too busy to hang out in Carter's loft," he said, giving me a knowing stare. Before I knew it, I felt a sharp pull on my shoulder until my back hit the steel locker behind me, hard. It was Josh.

"Whoa, man, Jesus," Ethan said, the pitch in his voice rising.

"What the fuck, Andie?" Josh said shakily. I knew he didn't want me talking to Ethan and there I was, behind his back. I couldn't understand why Josh was here in this hallway. I knew his schedule. I had been so careful. But it didn't matter. He was here, and I was pinned against a locker while he shoved his forearm tighter and tighter against my collarbone.

"I'm sorry," I said weakly. There was that word again.

"Dude, chill out," Ethan said, his expression changing from surprise to panic.

Josh whipped around, focusing his steely gaze on Ethan. "Stay out of our business, man. You don't want to mess with me." His voice was shaking.

Even though Ethan towered over Josh, he knew better and backed away, holding his hands up as if to say, "I give up."

The other students who had looked when they heard my back hit the locker had since looked away and continued going about their day. Maybe I was overdramatic about these incidents. If nobody else cared, why did I?

Just as quick as he arrived, Josh was gone, disappearing into a sea of students walking to their next class.

"What the hell was that, Andrea?" Ethan said frantically, reaching for me.

I pushed his extended arm away. "Nothing, don't worry about it. I'm sorry I bothered you." My voice was soft as I backed up, eventually turning and walking purposely to my next class. I saw Stephanie walking the opposite direction on my way, and I tried to look away so she wouldn't notice me.

"Hey, girl!" she shouted.

I forced a smile and kept walking.

She stopped, puzzled.

I heard Ethan call her name from down the hall and she headed toward him. I knew he was going to tell her what he saw, but I wished he wouldn't. Josh was right, it wasn't anyone else's business but ours, and I could take care of myself. Plus, Josh *loved* me, and this was complicated. Ethan couldn't possibly understand our relationship by seeing us for two minutes on a bad day.

I didn't cry this time. And I was proud of that. Maybe I was getting better at this. I wondered if Josh would notice. Maybe he would be proud of me, too.

Chapter Eleven

The next day was Saturday, the talent show, and I woke up sweating. I was so nervous for Josh that I couldn't concentrate on the day, so I floated around the house doing chores, finishing homework, and counting the seconds until it was time for Harper to pick me up. By the time she arrived, I had spent an hour teasing my hair and picking out the perfect outfit so Josh could feel proud to look out and see me in the crowd. I was frustrated at how the material of this new maxi-dress hung off of me, though. When I bought it last month, it had fit perfectly, making my waist appear small and hugging my hips just right, but today it felt like I was wearing a shapeless curtain.

It's just your nerves, I told myself. Josh will appreciate that you're trying.

I hopped into Harper's car, hoping she would comment on my appearance, or at least recognize my effort, but she just turned up the music and started talking.

"I heard Intentionally Blank plays every month in the quad at Michigan, so when I'm there next year, I'll get to see them all the time," she boasted, as I recognized their latest album playing from her speakers. "I heard Sloane is transferring there next year, so I'll probably see Carter all the time, too."

I felt like rolling my eyes. Was Harper trying to make me jealous? It wasn't working. I would never tell her this, but I knew that she wasn't even in the same ecosphere as Carter Wells, let alone in his league. She knew that, too.

"Sounds cool," I said dryly. Then I remembered how Carter had asked about me. I wouldn't dare tell

Harper, as she'd tell Josh for sure, and nothing good would come from that. It was my little secret that I let myself daydream about from time to time.

In these fantasies, I'd envision myself at the loft, watching the band practice. Carter would ask me how they sounded, genuinely caring about my response as he stared at me with those big, inquisitive eyes. The fantasy always ended the same way, with Carter realizing he couldn't live without me. But that kind of life and those kinds of guys never happened for people like me. There was always someone prettier, thinner, artsier. Always. And even if I were smarter and more interesting, the petite girls with perfect hair would beat me every time. Even though I knew I could adore Carter passionately and deeply, it didn't compare to Sloane's almond-shaped green eyes and flawless body. I had a curfew; she had an agenda. I'd never had a drink; she loved to party. I was a virgin; she was a goddess. There was never a competition to start. The odds were stacked so high I would've been laughed off the course had I entered. But I loved to fantasize. I would get lost in my thoughts, and it felt good that they lived safely inside me. Nobody, not even Josh, could take them or damage them or make them any less beautiful. It was only for me.

I had come back to reality by the time we arrived at the school.

"I'm so excited!" Harper exclaimed. "He's worked so hard for this. Let's sit in the front row. I promised him I'd be close enough so he could see me."

As we entered the auditorium, Harper made a dash for the last two seats up front, waving me over. I followed more slowly, taking in the surroundings, looking throughout the crowd to see who I recognized. Josh was backstage, I assumed, so I felt a bit free to converse lightly before the show started.

As I continued down the aisle, I felt a hand softly touch my shoulder. When I turned around, my mouth opened and I had to force myself to close it as I stared. It was Carter.

"Hey, Andrea," he said. We hadn't seen each other in months, not since that incident at the sandwich shop. This time I wanted to make a better impression. I needed to say something, and the longer I waited, the more awkward it got.

"Hi," I finally said.

"Long time no see. How you been?" Did he really care? Or was this some kind of prank?

"Good. What're you doing here?" I blurted out, realizing too late that that was probably a little blunt.

"Oh, maybe you heard that Ethan's drumming for my band now? Well he's performing tonight, so I thought we should support him. The guys are saving me a seat over there." He pointed near the stage.

"Cool. Yes, I did hear that. Ethan's a great drummer." I was unsure of where to go next. I was having a hard time thinking of words in his presence. Everything about him was perfect. Even his imperfections were perfect. He tucked a lock of thick brown hair behind his ear and gave me his trademark sexy half smile.

"Yeah, cool. Well, hey, I better get to my seat, but I'll see you around?" He focused his eyes as he looked at me. At that moment, I felt like he knew all of my secrets and saw through all of my daydreams. It was as if he figured me out with one look. And strangely, it felt good.

"Sure," I said, while my eyes begged him not to go. As he turned to leave, I took a deep breath, trying to decipher exactly what the room felt like with Carter Wells in it.

The lights flashed in the auditorium, and I hurried

to meet Harper in the front. I didn't think she'd seen me talking to Carter. There were too many people for her to have noticed. Plus, I was sure she would mention it if she had, and she didn't say a word. This was another secret that was all mine. I knew I would hold onto that brief exchange for a long time.

"Oh God, Carter and the band are here," she said, motioning to her left where they sat together, talking and laughing.

"Yeah, I saw." I tried not to sound as dreamy as I felt. I looked in their direction, Carter looked back. We locked eyes, just for a moment. He smiled and went back to his conversation. I filed that moment deep into my memory, making a mental note to reassess it later.

"I wonder if Josh knows that those guys are here," she said. I had spent several long minutes not thinking about Josh, and I felt a little guilty. When the lights dimmed, my guilt turned back to nervousness as I waited for the show to start. An acapella duo, a violinist, and a jazz singer all breezed through their sets on stage, and then it was Josh's turn as they wheeled out a piano.

Harper squeezed my knee in excitement.

"Ladies and gentlemen, please welcome to the stage, Josh McMillan, performing a David Bowie classic," the announcer boomed from the speakers. Everyone clapped politely; I wanted to cheer, but I was afraid of embarrassing him, so I tried to match the tempo of the room.

"Woo! Go, Josh!" Harper yelled, clapping louder than anyone.

Josh started playing, and when he began singing, I was distracted by Harper as she sat on the edge of her seat, mouthing every word. He sounded great, but I was having trouble focusing on anything other than Harper's enthusiasm.

I found myself growing angry as the song progressed—angry because it seemed clear that Harper still had feelings for Josh and angrier yet that I knew there was nothing I could do about it. If I confronted Josh, it would end in an angry incident. If I confronted Harper, she would deny it and tell Josh, which again, would lead to a hostile incident. There was no way this ended well for me, so I'd have to keep my mouth shut. All I could do was play this game that she was apparently telling me was in progress. But I had a head start. And she underestimated my desire to win.

When the song was over, Harper leaped to her feet, exploding in cheers and claps. I stood up, too, safely clapping in unison with the room. I tried to sneak a glance at Carter's reaction, but it was too dark to get a clear look.

Josh seemed pleased with himself. He nodded to the crowd, gave a quick wave, and exited the stage.

"He was unbelievable! Wasn't he *amazing*?" Harper said excitedly.

"Yes, he was great." And he was. But that melody didn't sit well with me after what happened last time I heard him attempt to play it. It was a beautiful song, but I couldn't appreciate it in the way I wanted to. I felt uneasy, and the nausea was building up again, even though I had only eaten a cup of soup and some raw carrots today, hoping the less I ate, the less sick I would feel. But apparently, that strategy wasn't working either.

I sat through the rest of the show, hoping each time someone new took the stage that it was the last performer. When it finally ended, Harper and I went out to the lobby, and my eyes feverishly searched for Carter in the crowd, figuring if anyone noticed they would assume I was looking for Josh. When I finally spotted Carter, I felt a tinge of excitement replace some of the building nausea, but then my heart sank again when I saw Sloane on his arm, laughing way too loudly at somebody's joke that was probably not that funny. I ducked behind a crowd before he caught my eye, and then I heard Harper's distinct laugh from across the room, so I made my way toward it to see her giving Josh a big hug while she jumped up and down.

"You were incredible! Everybody is talking about it. Seriously, you are so, so good. The best of the night by far!" She squealed, and he ate up every word, grinning wider than I'd ever seen before.

"Awesome set," I said as I got closer. "It was beautiful."

"Thanks, Andie." He gave me a quick side hug and kissed me on the cheek. "You look great tonight, by the way," he whispered. *Thank God.* My hard work had paid off. I wondered if Carter thought I looked great, too?

"We're celebrating!" Harper shouted. "Let's go grab some food. The night is young!" She'd never been this energetic before.

"Well, I have to get home for curfew," I said, knowing she was fully aware.

"Aw too bad, Andie, we can drop you off on the way." She tried to sound disappointed.

By the time I got home that night, I was fuming but kept trying harder and harder to swallow it as far down as I could. My parents were already asleep, so I crawled into bed, still fully dressed and made up, and just laid there, staring at the darkness. I started to play through the evening's events in my head, but my thoughts were interrupted by a ping from my phone. I grabbed it, hoping it was Josh, but was puzzled when I noticed an unfamiliar number.

I opened the message.

Carter: Hey, Andrea, it's Carter. Hope u don't mind, I asked Ethan for your #. Now you have mine too ;)

I almost dropped my phone. I let the excitement flood through me this time since I was alone and could enjoy every morsel of this feeling to myself. At that moment, I didn't care that nothing would or could ever happen, I didn't care that Sloane had perfect skin and long lashes, and I didn't care about Harper mouthing the words to "Space Oddity." I was in the moment for the first time in as long as I could remember. I was always plagued by worrying about what would happen next. It felt powerful to live directly in the moment, even if it was brief.

Me: Thx--good seeing you today.

I typed my response after waiting what felt like an appropriate amount of time between desperate and uninterested. I saved his number but quickly deleted the conversation. This was another moment that was just for me. And if there wasn't proof of it, nobody could ruin it, or point out its faults.

"Carter thinks about me sometimes," I said to myself out loud, just to hear what the words sounded like. And that fact would be enough to last me for a while. I drifted to sleep gently that night—not hyper-focused on analyzing the day's events, nor overly anxious about tomorrow's, but bathed in the immediate. Carter thought about me sometimes. And that, right now, was good enough.

Chapter Twelve

I didn't hear from Josh until late the next day, Sunday, when he invited me to come over to watch a movie. I was pretty sure that was code for messing around, and I didn't want to. Plus, I had to read ahead in my English Lit textbook since I'd be missing the first period tomorrow to finally go to the doctor's appointment my mom had set up. But I knew better, so I agreed to meet him after dinner.

When I arrived, he greeted me warmly. I didn't ask how his night was and he didn't offer. I thought it was better that way. I figured any story other than "I had a terrible time because I missed you too much" would be unsatisfying. Plus, I knew Josh well enough to know he wasn't a guy who liked being pressed for details he didn't entirely want to share, so I let it pass. We started talking about last night's talent show when his mother entered his bedroom, a basket of folded laundry in her arms.

"Oh, hi. Sorry I didn't know you had company," she said. Donna McMillan was a sweet, quiet woman who always looked exhausted. We'd never officially met though I had seen her before at school performances.

"Hi, Mrs. McMillan. I'm Andrea Cavanaugh. It's nice to meet you." I stood up, thinking that was the polite thing to do, but realized her arms were full with the laundry basket, so I didn't offer a handshake.

She gave a weak smile, and I awkwardly sat back down.

"Hi, dear. It's good to meet you, too, finally. Sorry to interrupt, but Josh, I wanted to make sure you had this before tomorrow." She nodded toward the laundry basket she was holding.

"Yeah, okay," Josh replied, standing up to take

the basket from her. "What in the actual hell, Mom?" he shouted when he looked at the top layer of neatly folded t-shirts. He dropped the basket to the ground and picked up his blue Bob Dylan shirt, which had several large bleach stains covering the logo. "This *was* my favorite shirt, and now it's ruined. Way to go, Mom. This was a classic. They don't even sell them anymore. You fucking idiot!"

She covered her face with her hands. "I'm so, so sorry Josh, that shirt must have gotten mixed in with a different load. It's my fault. I feel terrible."

"Well obviously it's your fault," he replied, looking at me and rolling his eyes. I was at a loss for how to respond. I couldn't agree with Josh and hurt his poor mother, but I couldn't stand up for her and be the next target of his anger, so I just sat frozen on the edge of his bed, hoping they'd both just forget I was there.

"I'm sorry, honey," she said again, seemingly very distraught. "I promise I'll make it up to you."

"Whatever, just get out." he said, walking toward her so she backed out of the doorway before he slammed the door.

"Sorry you had to see that. God, my mom's such an idiot, I swear," he said as if what had happened was an entirely normal mother-son moment.

"No worries," I said, pretending to be casual. I had never seen Josh talk to anyone other than me that way, and I hated to admit that it felt a little good to see I wasn't the only one.

"Anyway, where were we?" he said, revisiting our prior conversation as he ran through the list of last night's performers—the good, the bad, the terrible. And then he changed the discussion to the upcoming prom. We were not eligible to attend as juniors unless a senior invited us. That meant Harper was allowed to go, but neither of us had heard her mention it.

"Do you think she'll ask someone?" he asked.

"Oh, I don't know." I honestly hadn't thought much about it.

"She probably won't go. Harper's too good for something as stupid as prom," he decided. I was disappointed to hear his lack of enthusiasm for the event as I had already imagined us attending next year a hundred different times. How we'd wear matching colors and take silly pictures and hold each other close to the music while our friends all marveled that our relationship was still going strong after so long. His attitude was crushing my fantasy. I had dreamed of my senior prom since I was in middle school. But I had a year to warm him up to the idea.

"I mean, do you think she will?" he asked again. His voice sounded almost ... jealous? I decided to test the waters, slowly and safely.

"I don't know," I replied. "Maybe she'll ask Brandon or Jeff," I guessed, referring to the only other two guys I'd seen Harper easily converse with outside of Josh, Ethan, and Mr. Thompson.

"Oh, no way, those guys are losers. She only knows Brandon from calculus study group and Jeff from band, but she's his section leader, and he sucks at sax anyway." Josh seemed intent on figuring this out.

"Well, we can ask her tomorrow." I tried not to let my voice sound as annoyed as I was becoming.

"Yeah..." he said, getting lost in his thoughts for a moment before snapping out of it and stretching out on his bed, motioning for me to recline next to him. "Now, how about that movie?" He grinned.

I knew what he meant. I didn't want to feel his hand inside of me again. I was still sore from last time. But I figured it would hurt less than what would happen if I disagreed, and it would give me some close, intimate time to kiss him and be held before it escalated, which I wanted more than anything. So I laid down, closing my eyes while I expected him to kiss me.

But he didn't kiss me. I felt him unbutton my jeans and my heart sank. He skipped the kissing, the seduction part that I so loved, that part that left me feeling breathy and beautiful. Instead, he went right to the part I hated.

When he finished, I didn't feel desired. I felt used. And disgusting.

"Thanks, that was great," I lied.

"Oh, there's more where that came from." He shot me a devilish grin, which made me nervous.

"You know," I stammered, "I-I told you before, I'm not ready to go any farther. And I don't want to have sex," I confessed, surprised at how bluntly it came out. We had discussed this before, but I felt that it bore repeating after his comment. I cautiously waited for his response.

"Yeah, no shit. I'm just saying..." Josh's tone shifted to coy. "When you *are* ready, then I was born ready, baby." I hated how arrogant he sounded, and I had an urge to tell him how much I disliked every moment of him touching me, but I bit my tongue and forced a smile.

"I love you, Andie," he whispered, kissing me quickly on the lips.

A thrill ran through my spine when he said those words. I couldn't get enough of it. It was like a carrot he dangled in front of me, and just when I got too tired to keep running, he'd bring it out, and I would get my second wind.

Chapter Thirteen

The next morning, instead of driving to school, I met my mom at the doctor's office. She had made an appointment to get my stomach issues checked out. I knew I wasn't sick, but I figured it was easier to appease her by going to the appointment than it was to try and explain. When I entered the waiting room, she was already there, waving me over.

"Sorry you're going to be late for work." I shrugged. "I told you I could've come by myself."

"It's no worries. I want to be here. We need to figure out what's going on."

When the nurse called my name, my mom stood up, too, and started following me to the door.

"Really, Mom, you don't have to come back."

"Hush, just keep walking."

When we arrived in the small, chilly exam room, the nurse asked me to step on the scale. I slipped off my sandals and stood on it, feeling the cold, rough plastic under my bare feet.

When the number appeared on the screen, my mother gasped. "Andrea, you've lost fifteen pounds." There was a grave concern in her voice. "What is going on with you?"

The nurse jotted notes in my chart. "The doctor will be with you shortly," she said dryly, leaving the room.

I put my sandals back on and flopped onto the exam table, the white paper crinkling underneath me as I scooted back.

"Are you *trying* to lose weight? Because you don't need to," my mother offered.

"No," I said honestly. I wasn't trying, though I

didn't mind the fact that I'd lost a few pounds. Knowing that there was now less of my body in the world felt eerily comforting. "But come on, it's not like I couldn't stand to lose some." I grabbed my shrinking love handles to prove my point.

"Stop that." She lightly slapped my hand away from my hips.

We were interrupted by a quick knock at the door followed by Dr. Adams entering.

"Hello, ladies, to what do I owe the pleasure of having not one but two of the Cavanaugh women in my office today?" he said loudly, pulling up a rolling stool. He was tall, middle-aged, with bushy eyebrows and a warm smile. He'd been our family doctor for years and was nice, though sometimes tried too hard to be funny.

"Andrea can't keep anything down. She's rarely hungry, and apparently has lost fifteen pounds over the last six or so months," my mom said sharply.

I looked down, unsure of what to say. They didn't understand. "She's overreacting," I stated. "I lost weight, but it's not like I was underweight to start. My stomach has been upset lately. I'm not trying to lose weight." I was afraid of the direction this conversation was going in.

"Andrea," Dr. Adams said, rolling his stool closer to me and pushing his small square glasses to the top of his head as if he was about to say something serious, which I dreaded. "Are you vomiting on purpose? After meals?"

I groaned. "No! I swear that's not what this is about. Mom, come on, you know me better than that."

"I don't know, Andrea," she said softly, shaking her head. "You haven't been yourself lately." It was the first time I'd seen her look this worried since this had all started. I hated that I was doing this to her. I needed to do a better job of hiding my stress about Josh, because I never intended for this to affect anyone else. I had probably been too moody at home, especially in the days after the incidents, so I vowed to myself in that moment that I would adopt a poker face of steel from now on. That way nobody else would get hurt. My mom, my dad, Dr. Adams, Stephanie, Ethan, none of them could comprehend my feelings for Josh. It was complicated and sensitive. *He* was complicated and sensitive. And by loving him, I was helping him. And they wouldn't understand.

"I'm sorry, Mom. I'm probably just stressed. You know finals are coming up, and I have to start thinking about applying to college next year. It's just a lot. With school and the band, I'm just overwhelmed."

"Stress is a common cause of digestive issues," Dr. Adams stated calmly. "But to be safe, let's get some blood work to rule out anything more serious." He stood up and opened the drawer of the desk in the corner, shuffling through some items until he pulled out a couple of pamphlets on eating disorders in teens, handing one to me and one to my mom.

I rolled my eyes. "Dr. Adams, I swear—"

He interrupted. "Now now, just take a look through these and see if you identify with any of these symptoms and if so just call my office. We can recommend an excellent program."

"Honestly, that won't be necessary," I said, trying to hand the pamphlet back to him before my mom grabbed it from my hand, shoving both into her purse.

"Thank you for your time, doctor," she said. "We'll be on the lookout for a call about her blood test results."

He nodded.

After the nurse drew my blood, my mom and I

made our way to the parking lot, neither of us knowing what to say so we just let the tension hang thick in the air.

When we reached my car, she hugged me tightly. "It's going to be okay," she said, obviously unsure of what the "it" even was.

"I know, Mom. Honestly it's fine." I desperately wanted to drive far, far away from this conversation. "I'm gonna be late. I need to make it in time for the second period at least." I opened the car door.

"Okay, I love you," she said, her mouth pursed into a straight, firm line while I felt her eyes study me, analyzing my demeanor.

"Love you too." I climbed into the driver's seat and waved goodbye as I pulled out of the parking lot, shaking my arms quickly as if that could get this morning off of my skin.

I told myself it *would* be okay. I would try harder. I would get better at this. I didn't want anyone to worry, especially my mom. If anything, I wanted them to be happy for me, and I hated that it seemed like nobody was. Hadn't they been to the talent show? Hadn't they seen what a prodigy Josh was? And *he* chose *me*. I didn't know why that was so hard for people to understand. At least Harper seemed to get it. She knew how special Josh was. But of course, the one person who understood was the one person I couldn't talk to about it. I turned on the radio, letting the commercials and airy pop songs tune out my internal dialogue.

When I got to school, I tried out my new strategy. I just sat and listened. I took notes in class, I smiled back at people who smiled at me, I answered questions when I was called on, but I otherwise just existed. I just took up space, floating through the halls, sitting in desks. And it was ... easy, comfortable. And at this point, that felt like a win. Nobody got upset, nobody was worried, nobody was bothered. And that was a very welcome change.

When the last bell rang, I gathered up my books and headed to the band room, getting ready for practice.

Ethan was already there and nodded when he saw me, but didn't get up or say anything. Maybe Ethan wasn't laughing and smiling, but he also wasn't hurting or angry, so I counted his expressionless nod as a success. He probably didn't realize it then, but I knew that the less he cared about me, the easier his life would be. It was becoming clearer and clearer that I was constantly a cause of anxiety and frustration for the people I cared about. And Ethan didn't deserve that.

I opened my backpack and pretended to sort through some things to cut the awkwardness in the room where just Ethan and I sat in silence. When a few others filed in and it felt safe to relax again, I sat down near the front of the room and studied the sheet music we'd been working on.

When Harper came in, she set her saxophone case on a chair and skipped toward me in a silly fashion, beaming. "Hi there," she said in a singsong voice.

"Whoa, somebody is peppy," I replied. "What's going on?"

Josh entered the room and headed toward us.

"I asked Brandon to prom, and he said ... *yes*." She shouted the last word.

"That's awesome!" I was genuinely relieved. Maybe this would get her off of Josh's constant radar a little bit.

"Wait, what?" Josh said, hurrying closer.

"Brandon is going to be my prom date," Harper said again, enjoying each word.

"Brandon Kessler? Honestly? Oh, come on, Harper," Josh said, rolling his eyes. "That guy sucks."

"He does not!" she replied sternly.

"You barely even know him," Josh said back. I was beginning to feel uneasy at how jealous he sounded. I wanted to say something, but I remembered my new strategy, and I stayed quiet. If I told Harper I was happy for her, Josh would be mad. If I told Josh I agreed with him, then Harper would be angry. There was no winning scenario, so I just sat and listened. Watching. Existing.

"Josh, what do you even care?" Harper asked. That got my attention. I wanted to know the answer too. I held my breath, waiting to hear his reply. I envied Harper for being able to talk to him however she wanted.

"I *don't* care. I just think you can do better than Brandon Kessler."

"Well, it sounds like you care," Harper challenged.

Mr. Thompson walked in, breaking up the conversation.

"All right, let's take our seats," he said, approaching the podium. When the rustling quieted, he cleared his throat. "As you guys know, our invitational is next week."

There were a couple of cheers from the group. The invitational was everybody's favorite performance because there were schools from all over the state that came to perform, and the auditorium was usually packed. Plus, there were tons of vendors and food and music throughout the day. It was always fun, and our band got to showcase our favorite songs from the year. "So if anyone can't attend, you need to let me know ASAP so we can get an alternate. And you can expect our practices to run a little late over the next few days while we prep. Now let's get started. Andrea?" He motioned for me to take my conducting position at the podium.

Josh seemed distracted during practice. I tried not

to focus too much on him as I directed, but I couldn't help it. I reminded myself that next year would be *our* turn at prom, so I tried to refocus my mind on the music.

Chapter Fourteen

By the time the invitational rolled around, I thought my new strategy had been working well. I'd been forcing myself to eat more in front of my mom so she wouldn't worry as much, and if nausea took over and it had to come back up, I was much stealthier and able to get it over with quickly and quietly so as not to bother my parents.

But then it happened. I hesitated during our performance, only for a second, but long enough to cause Josh's piano solo to start late. My heart leaped into my throat. He glared at me briefly as he rushed to catch up with the melody, but it was enough. I got the message. I didn't want the performance to end. I didn't want to walk off the stage and face what I had done. I had been careless, and I knew better.

Moments later, I was crouched by the cold, steel lockers while Josh screamed.

"Why did you do that, Andrea?" he said, his voice unnervingly shaky and piercingly loud.

Instinctively, I drew my hands to my head, clasping my fingers together like a meaningless shield while I buried my face in the false safety of my arms. I tucked my knees against my chest as I waited for this latest incident to end.

"It'll be over soon," I told myself through scattered thoughts. And once it was over, my breath would return and I could stumble my way to the next incident where my heart would just end up back in my throat. I lived for those uneventful moments between incidents. Until then, I would just close my eyes, breathe, and exist.

I slowly opened one eye to see Josh's face turning

red as he shouted at me. I noticed a crowd forming. But Josh was oblivious and threw his hands wildly while he continued. He grabbed a hardcover music book out of an onlooker's grasp and threw it toward me. I felt the bookend thud against my forearm, which was still shielding my head. Another book fell at my feet, sprawling open on the tile floor. And then came another, its sharp corner stabbing my forearm as I attempted to defend my face.

The hallway was eerily quiet, Josh's angry voice being the only noise breaking the awkward, heavy silence. Nobody else moved. The crowd was frozen, collectively unsure of what to do, but I didn't expect intervention anymore. I had heard the whispers. Despite the anti-bullying posters that littered the Oakwood High hallways, any conflict between couples was typically deemed "relationship drama" or "none of my business," if anything at all.

Finally, after several seemingly endless minutes, I noticed a break in the crowd as a figure started pushing his way to the front. I shifted my head up straight to see and braced myself for whatever was to come next. It was Mr. Thompson, hurrying through the crowd, his eyes glued to a still-screaming Josh.

In my mind, I silently begged Mr. Thompson to just turn around and let Josh blow off his steam. Tightly clenching my eyes shut, I imagined for a moment that I wasn't here. I was not here in this hallway, I was not here in this world, and I briefly got lost in the fantasy of how much better that would be for everyone. But I snapped back to the moment when Josh's brash voice turned into a pained, unfamiliar tone.

I opened my eyes to find Mr. Thompson gripping Josh's arms behind his back while he protested. Forcing Josh to his knees and eventually to the floor, Mr.

Thompson overpowered him, finally planting a knee into Josh's back while he firmly held his arms.

Josh screamed, and my reaction was to reach for him. I was concerned and protective and I hated myself for that.

"Don't hurt him!" I said as the life reentered my body in one sudden breath.

Mr. Thompson darted his eyes toward me while he tightened his grip on Josh. An audible gasp was heard from the crowd, and I felt a strong tug on my arm.

That's when Ethan dragged me briefly away from the chaos and embraced me in a way I barely knew I needed. When my breath steadied and my heartrate slowed, I left Ethan in that empty hallway and readied myself to face the aftermath of the latest incident.

When I returned, it was as if nothing had happened. Students and parents were milling about, chatting, waiting for the next band to hit the stage and perform.

"Hey, you!" My shoulders immediately tensed. "Where you been?" Josh asked, roughly wrapping his arm around my waist and flashing me a coy smile. "You ready for dinner, babe? I invited Harper to come, too. She's waiting in the parking lot." My body impulsively retreated from his grasp, but I forced it back toward him, knowing he'd sense that reaction as a sign of disrespect. So I swallowed the discomfort instead.

It was over for now, that incident in the hallway, and I could tell by the new tone in his voice that we would never talk about it again.

As we made our way to the exit, I saw Mr. Thompson standing outside an empty classroom. I hoped he would just allow us to pass by unannounced, letting the incident disappear into the air like so many others took comfort in doing. But when he saw us, he playfully slapped Josh on the shoulder.

"Sorry, brother," Mr. Thompson said with an awkward chuckle.

"Oh, it's all good, man! We'll see ya in a bit, going to grab dinner," Josh replied, pushing his fist out, which Mr. Thompson met with a friendly bump.

The harsh truth flooded over me. Nobody was going to help me. This was just my life now. I swallowed hard and choked back the tears that welled up as that realization sunk in.

There we were, Josh and I, with Harper as she drove toward my favorite Mexican restaurant. I sat in the back while they chatted and laughed, but I didn't know what about. I was just trying to breathe, focus, and prepare myself to have a regular dinner. A dinner where I wouldn't click my teeth against the metal fork, a dinner where I would pretend that I couldn't feel the bruise forming on my arm or the papercuts stinging my shoulder. And I'd even try not to let their inside jokes bother me. I bit my lip, hard, to keep the tears back while I stared out the car window, watching houses and shrubs pass.

By the time we arrived, I hadn't said a word, and nobody seemed to notice, which I think I preferred. Harper and Josh didn't skip a beat as they stepped out of the car, engrossed in a conversation about which Pink Floyd song was the best of all time. I wondered if they'd even care if I stayed in the car. Would they go about their dinner without me? Would one of them eventually say, "Oh, hey, didn't Andrea come with us?" And if they did, what would the other's response be? Figuring it was safer to join them than it was to be called out for something that could've been portrayed as defiant or sulky, I quietly opened the car door and followed, a few steps behind them.

As I made my way into the restaurant, I felt my phone vibrate in my pocket, so I snuck it out just enough so I could quickly look at the screen. It was Carter.

Carter: Are u ok?

I quickly turned my phone off and shoved it back into my pocket as I felt the tears well up again, but swallowed hard as if to push them deep into my body where I could access them at a safer, future moment. Carter's text haunted me throughout the entire dinner. The image of the blue bubble with the words "Are u okay?" neatly sprawled across my screen stuck in my head. How did he know? Either Ethan told him or Carter was there. Had he seen what happened? Were people talking about it? Either way, it was humiliating. I had been living in this perfect fantasy where Carter Wells thought I was interesting and spirited and cool, even. But now that idea was cracking as the realization that Carter knew I was just another vulnerable, pathetic girl who couldn't stand up to her angry, young boyfriend. He wouldn't understand, and we weren't nearly close enough for me to try and explain.

When the server came to our table, she asked if we were ready to order. Josh ordered tacos, Harper a burrito, and I hadn't even looked at the menu. All food sounded disgusting. I couldn't fathom enjoying a single bite.

"Um, I'll just have a cup of the tortilla soup," I said, thinking it'd look odd if I ordered nothing.

"Whoa call the press," Harper said jokingly. "Andrea's not getting enchiladas? Andie, we came here because it's your favorite."

"Sorry, I just want soup right now." I wished she had expressed something other than annoyance at my order. Worry, perhaps? Concern? But no, just frustration.

"We could've gone somewhere closer to the

school if we knew you didn't want to come here," Josh said, handing his menu to the server. "Bring us a plate of the veggie enchiladas, too. No soup." The server nodded and walked toward the kitchen. I looked down. "Come on, Andie. I know you're watching your figure, but live a little!" Josh said.

I nodded.

"Watching your figure? What does *that* mean?" Harper asked.

"Haven't you noticed how good my girl looks lately?" Josh boasted, scooting his chair closer to me and putting his hands around my waist and squeezing.

I felt my skin flinch but tried to overpower my reaction by faking a laugh.

"Are you on a diet or something?" Harper asked.

"No, just trying to be healthy," I lied.

She turned her head, but I caught her rolling her eyes as she turned. I didn't care. I knew she was just feeling self-conscious. Josh was making all of us feel awkward, but he didn't seem to catch on.

"Honestly, it seems like every week someone is telling me how good you look," Josh said, eyeing me up so that I could feel his thoughts and wanted nothing more than to wash them off of me.

"Can you guys believe prom is next week?" Harper interjected, clearly trying to change the subject. "And then graduation? And then I'm outta here."

"You're so lucky," Josh replied. "I can't believe we're stuck here another year. This place really is the worst."

"Cheers to that." Harper smiled, raising her Diet Coke.

When the food came, my stomach was so twisted and knotted that I wanted to vomit just at the sight of it. I sat staring at my enchiladas, knowing that there was no way I'd be able to keep them down, but also knowing I'd have to make an effort for show. I cut one with my fork and slowly pushed some of the food around, making space between the rice and tortillas. I took a small bite, making sure to guard my teeth with my lips so as not to make a noise with my fork, and didn't even taste it. The flavors that once used to excite me, that I used to crave, just felt like paper in my mouth. I swallowed and felt my stomach turn. I could probably manage to do this a few more times at best, so I would have to be better at creating an illusion on my plate as I maneuvered things around, trying to create as much space as possible.

"Are we going to the Intentionally Blank show next week?" Harper asked as she chewed. "The one where they're introducing Ethan?"

"Eh, those guys are overrated," Josh said in between bites of chips.

I suddenly realized that I hadn't replied to Carter's text, and probably wouldn't have a chance to until much later when I was alone. What would I even say? "Sorry you saw my boyfriend have a meltdown and attack me, but don't worry, everything's good?" I was getting tired of making excuses, but I didn't have a choice. Nobody else seemed to think it was a big deal, unless ... what if Mr. Thompson talked to my parents about what happened? Would he do that? If he did, they'd probably forbid me from seeing Josh again, but I didn't know how to feel about that. Was I ready to give up on love? To let go of what could be my only chance at having someone care about me? I couldn't decide, and I felt so exhausted that I didn't have the energy to focus on what *could* happen. I just needed to get through each moment. I would reply to Carter later when it was safe. He was probably just being cordial, anyway. He barely knew me. He was just a good guy doing the right thing by checking on the sad, wounded deer. I convinced myself that he didn't really care. He was probably somewhere with Sloane right now, being beautiful, being charming, doing something glamorous.

When Josh and Harper finished their meals and pushed their plates aside, I decided I'd made enough of a dent in my dinner for it to be considered passable. As I sat back in my chair, I felt my five barely digested bites heaving in the back of my throat, my stomach cramping. I excused myself to the bathroom, hoping Harper wouldn't follow me, but then remembering she would cherish the alone time with Josh.

When I got closer to the bathroom, I quickened my gate and was narrowly able to fling the stall door open before I started retching. I dropped to my knees and gripped the side of the toilet, knowing in the back of my mind how filthy it was, but trying to focus on just getting this over with. When it was finally out, I weakly stood up, wiped my mouth with a square of toilet paper, and flushed, praying nobody else had been in a nearby stall listening to me. I hadn't been able to keep that one as quiet as I'd been practicing at home, so I was grateful when I exited the stall and didn't see any feet under the swinging metal doors. I splashed some water on my face and gargled it, popping a breath mint from my purse that I kept for these very occasions. I wiped some tears that were pushed out when my body heaved. Then I forced a smile and walked back out into the dismal world I had created for myself. I was as ready as I could be to face the next moment, and the next, and the next.

On the drive back to the school, my insides felt empty and throbbing. I couldn't tell if I was hungry anymore. It all blended—the nausea, the discomfort, the anxiety. Luckily, we were done performing for the night. We now just had to finish out the invitational by attending the end-of-year awards ceremony. I didn't speak on the car ride home and wasn't spoken to, either.

When we got back, we settled into a corner on the floor of the gym as we waited for the final event to begin. I saw Ethan walking across the floor with some other guys from our band. When he saw me cuddled up next to Josh, I could see the heartbreak in his eyes when he shook his head, as if to say, "what are you doing?" But he didn't get it. Ethan didn't say anything, nor did he come over. He sat down with his friends a few rows away from us.

I fought the urge to make eye contact.

"Thank you, everyone, for coming tonight." Mr. Thompson's voice boomed through the speakers as he stood alone on the stage holding a microphone. "It's been a great invitational, and we've seen some exceptional talent tonight." I guess the incident from earlier had left his mind, since just a couple hours before he was literally holding Josh back from a violent fit, and now he was casually addressing the audience as he saw Josh firmly plant his arm around me in the crowd. Mr. Thompson's candor only echoed my greatest fear: nobody cared.

"Our first award tonight is our VIP award that we give every year to our most valuable musician. This year, I'm honored to present it to somebody who not only is an incredible, natural talent but who I'm sure will put our little jazz band on the map next year as there've already been rumblings about him from the top music institutions in the state! Please welcome to the stage, the incomparable Josh McMillan."

Josh stood up so quickly I had to catch myself from falling backward. Stunned, though I shouldn't have been surprised, I clamored to my feet and clapped as he jogged up to the stage, a huge grin on his face.

"Wow!" Harper exclaimed in my ear, trying to

talk over the cheers from the room. "I don't think this award has ever gone to someone who wasn't a senior. I'm so excited for him!"

I nodded, smiling, and did feel truly happy for his success. He deserved it. Nobody was better than Josh when it came to musical talent, and now it was official. And I reminded myself that *he* chose *me* to be with, which struck a new spark in me to keep working on our relationship. When someone this well-respected and decorated chooses you, it's an honor. And I had to remember that. Plus, he was a genius, everybody knew that, so maybe his mind worked differently than most. Look at all the famous, iconic musicians out there. The more loved their music was, the more they resembled the stereotypical tortured artist. So maybe my purpose was to be the woman behind the man who changed the world? Elvis had Priscilla. John had Yoko. Kurt had Courtney. Hell, even The Plain White T's had whoever Delilah was.

Yes, I was doing the right thing, I told myself, while Josh posed for pictures with Mr. Thompson and his gold trophy that was shaped like an eighth note.

When Josh came off the stage, he hugged me and spun me around, giving me a big kiss, before accepting congratulations and shoulder pats from Harper and the other band members sitting near us. And just like that, it felt like the day's prior incident had disappeared from everybody's mind. Even Ethan looked like he'd forgotten as he clapped for Josh and chatted with friends. But I hadn't. I tried to push it far back in my mind, but I could only get it so far. I knew it could come flooding back at any moment if I wasn't careful. So I would have to be careful.

Chapter Fifteen

That Monday, back at school, nothing seemed out of the ordinary. Nobody looked at me differently, nobody talked to me differently, so I was sure that the spectacle of our incident during the invitational was behind us. That was until Stephanie showed up outside my English class after third period.

"Oh, hey, Steph. What're you doing here?" I knew she was usually on the other side of the school at this time.

"I came to talk to you," she said plainly. Her usually bright eyes were fixed on me and blanketed in worry. She had dark eyes that she regularly hid with emerald green contacts. It was kind of her signature, so it was a bit eerie to see them look so somber.

"Oh okay." I gathered my books together as I prepared to walk to my next class.

"Andrea, I heard about this weekend."

"What about it?" I said, knowing exactly what she meant.

"I heard what Josh did to you. And honestly, I'm just ... disgusted."

I started walking down the hall, assuming she'd walk with me, but instead, she grabbed my arm and stopped me. "This is serious, Andie. What the hell are you doing?"

"Jesus," I said, pulling my arm back. "It's not a big deal. I messed up our performance, and he was pissed, but then he got over it, and it's fine now."

"It's *not* fine." Her loud voice caused a few heads to turn. She pulled me into the attached hallway that was less crowded so she could talk more candidly. "It's not fine," she said again, quieter. "I didn't know this was going on. How *long* has this been going on?"

"How long has *what* been going on?" I challenged, feeling itchy and uncomfortable, wanting just to stop this conversation and crawl out of my skin.

"How long has he been ... has he been ... is he hurting you?" she whispered.

"No," I lied, wanting to go into more detail but not knowing how. "How did you hear about that anyway? You weren't even there."

"It doesn't matter how I heard about it. But it's messed up, okay?" Her famously green eyes started tearing up, and her voice broke. "Look, I love you, and I'm sorry I haven't been there. I thought you were just wrapped up in this relationship, and I know I've been busy too, but you're my oldest friend, and I'm always here for you."

"Thanks." I appreciated her sentiment, but I wished she would let it go. It would be easier for both of us if she did. She didn't know what she was stepping into. This was complicated, and it couldn't be boiled down to one event that she heard about secondhand. "But I'm all right."

"Andrea, I don't believe you." She tried to make eye contact which I avoided, not wanting to get pulled into the emotion of it. It was easier, safer, to just let these negative feelings wash over me, and then I could come back up for air when they were gone. I knew there wasn't anything Stephanie could do, so I didn't see the point in discussing it.

"Steph, I'm sorry that I'm upsetting you, but honestly, we're okay. When we're alone, Josh is really sweet. It's just that not everyone sees that side of him." I hoped she would believe me.

"Okay, just ... just call me if you need anything. Can you at least do that? Just promise me that you'll reach out if you need me." She reached for a hug, and I let her hug me. I thought it would make her feel better.

"Okay," I said. "I'm going to be late for class. I need to go." I took a deep breath and turned to walk away, feeling Stephanie's green eyes on my back, but knowing I was doing her a favor by not letting her get involved, whether she realized it or not.

When I got to the classroom and sat down, I tried to erase the conversation with Stephanie from my memory. To get myself in a better place, I went to the spot I always went to in my mind when I needed to feel good: Carter. The fantasy always started with him coming to my house one day unannounced, professing his undying love for me. Then I'd hold his perfect face in my hands, tuck a lock of his perfect brown hair behind his ear, and kiss him boldly on his perfect lips. There'd be such a passion that he'd know we were meant to be. As I zoned into this daydream, I felt my mouth curl into a smile, and then a shock ran through my body as I remembered his text. I had never responded. "Are u okay?" it had said. And I never replied. I pulled my phone out on my desk, staring at the screen. I only had a couple of minutes before class started, so I had to think quick.

I was at a loss for what to write back. I didn't know if I should apologize for taking so long to reply or play it cool as if I just now saw his text. The teacher walked into the room, and I had to respond now, because next was lunch and I couldn't be texting Carter, or any guy, in front of Josh. I typed out a hasty reply.

Me: Sorry. I'm okay. How are you?

I hit send and pushed my phone back deep into my pocket as class started, but I couldn't concentrate. I don't know why I cared so much about what I did or didn't say to Carter Wells. It wasn't like anything would or could ever happen. But I think it just felt good to know that I entered his mind sometimes. It made me feel somehow more legitimate, as a person, and like my fantasies weren't so incredibly far-fetched.

A few minutes into class, I felt the familiar vibrate of a new text message from my pocket. I winced, knowing I couldn't look at it until class was over, but I was dying to know what it said. Maybe Carter had said "Cool, let's hang out and talk about it," or "I broke up with Sloane, can I see you?" Until I actually looked at the phone, I told myself those were actual possibilities. If I didn't look at it, those options still existed, floating around in the atmosphere somewhere. But once I looked at it, whatever it said, whether "I've always loved you" or "Who are you again?" I would have to live with it. So I would take these next forty-five minutes as the opportunity to revel in the possibilities instead of being buried under my anxiety.

But when class ended, I grabbed my phone and set it on my desk. I took one last breath in the world where it was possible that Carter Wells could've sent me a love note, and then opened the text and braced myself for impact into the real world again.

Carter: Great—see you at my show next week?

But I knew I wasn't going to that show. It was Ethan's debut with Intentionally Blank, and I really wanted to attend, but Josh wasn't going, so I wasn't going.

Me: Idk, hope so but might be busy.

I hurriedly wrote back. Then I turned my phone off as I walked toward lunch, not wanting to have Carter's response come in while I was with Josh and Harper. Josh would be unnecessarily threatened, Harper would be unnecessarily jealous, and neither of them would understand that Carter was just being polite in between his loft parties and road trips with his hot girlfriend.

I smiled when I saw Josh waiting for me.

"Hi," I said. "Is Harper coming?"

"She's having lunch with Brandon today ... whatever." He sounded disappointed.

"Oh okay, maybe they're talking about prom plans."

"Yeah, obviously, but I don't care. She can hang out with that loser if she wants. I wanted some alone time with you anyway." He wrapped his hands around my waist. His light mood gave me instant relief. I was excited to spend time with *this* Josh.

"Let's get out of here," he whispered in my ear.

"Okay, Subway? Or that deli down the road?" I asked, suggesting nearby places we could grab lunch.

"I was thinking ... my house?" he asked. I smiled and nodded, hoping he was just interested in a quick make out session before coming back to school. I knew better, though. But I decided to play the same game I had played while I waited for Carter's text. For the ten minutes it would take to drive to Josh's house, I could pretend like there were other possibilities of what would happen. Maybe we really *would* just make out. Maybe it'd be magical and beautiful. Maybe it'd be a moment that was so heartfelt we'd talk about it for years. I let myself think that throughout the whole drive, even when he slipped his hand onto my thigh and rubbed my leg while he drove and even when he said he couldn't wait to put his hands on me. I just focused on the world that existed until proven otherwise.

When we got to his house, he walked quickly to his bedroom and I followed closely, compliantly. Without saying a word, he pulled my shirt over my head and tossed it on the floor amidst a pile of his dirty clothes. He motioned for me to lay down on his bed and climbed in next to me. I felt cold, exposed, and his sheets were scratchy. He pulled my pants down to my knees and I turned my head away from him, staring at the wall, trying to transfix my gaze on a piece of blue, peeling paint near the ceiling. I couldn't pretend anymore that a different world existed. Those ten minutes were over. We didn't make out. It was not magical or beautiful. He wasn't gentle, and I wasn't swept away by romance and attraction. I'd have to save that fantasy for next time. So I let him touch me and counted the seconds in my head while I stared at that patch of paint. When I got to two hundred and fifty-five seconds, he stood up and unbuckled his belt.

"What are you doing?" I said, a panic in my voice, knowing my resistance could be met with anger but needing an answer.

"Relax, I'm not going to put it in." He pulled his corduroys off, letting them fall to the carpet and then joined me back on the bed. He started rubbing himself against my leg while he touched me. I hated the way it felt, warm and firm, pressing at my smooth skin beneath the fabric of his boxers. I got to second three hundred and two when he pulled his underwear down slightly, just enough to expose the top of his penis.

"Touch it," he whispered, his eyes closed. I froze. This was the first time I had seen one in real life. It was ugly, unnatural looking. I wanted nothing to do with it, let alone to touch it. But I steadied my shaky hand and touched the tip with my index finger, closing my eyes tight.

Three hundred and three … three hundred and four … three hundred and five… I restarted the counting in my head, getting through the moment, knowing it would end soon so we could get back to school. He put his hand over mine and directed it up and down his shaft.

"Good girl."

Three hundred and six ... three hundred and seven ... three hundred and eight...

"I knew you'd be good at this."

Three hundred and nine ... three hundred and ten ... three hundred and eleven....

"Faster."

Three hundred and twelve ... three hundred and thirteen ... three hundred and fourteen ... three hundred and fifteen... I counted another twenty seconds until he finished and I pulled back. I sat up on the bed, covering my bare legs with the comforter, disgusted with every cell of my body. He let out a deep, satisfied sigh and leaped up, pulling his corduroys back on before snatching my clothes from the ground and throwing them at me without making eye contact. The hollow nausea was starting to overwhelm me.

"Get dressed. Meet me upstairs," Josh snapped, his tone completely changed from moments before.

I stayed frozen for a minute, my clothes in my lap, my face flushed with anger. I didn't know how much longer I could keep pretending that I wanted his rough, callused fingers inside of me, or his thick, ugly shaft sliding between my fingers. Maybe it was time I said something. Maybe Stephanie was right, and this wasn't normal. The very little I knew about sex had come from Steph when she would boast about her antics with her boyfriend, Nick. She always made it sound exciting, like it was something to envy, so maybe something really *was* wrong, because I felt awful. I took a deep breath and decided that Josh had crossed a line, and I would tell him. And if he hit me, then so be it. But I couldn't keep living in this fear and not wanting my own boyfriend to touch me.

This wave of relief fell over me as I washed my hands in the bathroom. And then I remembered that my phone was off, and when I turned it on, I'd probably have a message from Carter. And that was something to be excited about. If I have this conversation with Josh now, it might be a tough few days, but the more I thought about it while I got dressed, the more I felt like Josh didn't even really *like* me, let alone love me, so maybe he wouldn't be upset. Maybe he'd be relieved, too, and we'd just agree to part ways amicably. And I would go to Carter's show, and he'd see me in the crowd and kiss me in the alley behind the venue. And he'd never know that I'd been violated by this angry piano prodigy in a tie-dyed shirt. And we could pretend that when Carter touched me, gently and softly, it was my first time. As I pulled my shirt over my head and walked toward the stairs, my confidence grew with each step.

"You ready?" Josh said, waiting for me in the kitchen as he finished the sandwich he'd made for himself.

"Ready," I chirped, surprising myself with my new voice. I practically skipped to the car as I thought about what my future could hold. Even if I never found someone to love me again, that had to be better than feeling the way I'd been feeling. Maybe I could even enjoy food again, and talk to Ethan for hours on end about our favorite drummers as we would laugh and guess what college would be like.

As we got in the car, Josh was silent as he started the engine, pulling out of the driveway. It was now or never. Harper wasn't here to interrupt us, and if I waited much longer I could lose this newfound motivation, so I had to do it. Now.

"Josh..." I started, pushing through my anxiety and trying to hold my focus. "I've been thinking..."

"Ha, well there's a first." He groaned, making this conversation suddenly much easier.

"Sometimes I feel ... I kinda think ... I just, sometimes..." I was stammering. I had to get through this, like ripping off a bandage.

"Sometimes ... buh-buh-buh." He mocked me, exaggerating my stutter. His attitude gave me the rush I needed.

I took a deep breath. "I think we should break up."

Chapter Sixteen

I paused, waiting for a reaction, of which there was none. His face remained unchanged as he drove.

"I *want* to break up," I said, correcting my first statement, adding more power to the words.

Josh continued his silence, just staring at the road and blinking while he drove. It was eerie. The air felt thick, and my confidence began to shake, so I defaulted to breaking the painful silence with my voice.

"It's just ... sometimes I don't think you even like me. And we're both going to college in a year, and I just, I feel like *you'd* be happier without having to deal with me anymore." I said quickly.

His eyes squinted slightly as he focused, hard, on the windshield. I started squirming in my seat, trying to find a more comfortable position, but there was none. I couldn't tell if he was mad or relieved, and that was almost more frightening. I decided to stop talking. It was his turn now. But he didn't take the bait.

"Well ... what do you think?" I asked nervously. We were only five minutes away from the school.

He shook his head, letting out a soft laugh.

I tried frantically to read his expression, but it was such a gray line between joy and rage that my anxiety grew deeper as I felt an alarming tingle down my spine.

Josh looked over his shoulder—the road was empty—and he suddenly jerked the steering wheel as far as it would go, making a screeching U-turn.

"Jesus! Josh! Slow down!" I shouted, gripping the center console with my left hand and the inside of the passenger door with my right hand.

He swerved into a neighboring street that I didn't

recognize and picked up speed, a wild look in his eyes.

"You dumb bitch," he said, each word growing louder and more distinct. "You really think *you* can break up with *me*?" He started laughing, an almost maniacal laugh that you'd hear from a supervillain in a bad summer movie. "Okay, Andrea, let's think this through. You break up with me, and then what? Who's gonna want you now, hmm? Or haven't you thought that far?"

His words hurt, but I couldn't focus on a reaction while he was driving so fast, whipping around these neighborhood corners and finally pulling onto the interstate when he saw the opportunity. I didn't know exactly where we were, but I knew we were getting farther away from the school.

"Hey, why don't you slow down?" I offered, as calmly as I could, hoping he would sense some kind of comfort from my tone. "Let's just get back to school or just go somewhere and talk."

"We *are* talking," he screamed. "And we're not going anywhere until we establish something."

"Okay." My voice was beginning to shake. "But please just slow down." I closed my eyes tightly, fighting back the tears and trying to stay calm so as not to escalate the mood even more.

"Shut the fuck up!" His voice started breaking. He turned his head sharply, looking deep into my eyes. I didn't recognize him, his once playful eyes were red and filled with rage, and he had tear stains on his face that he wiped roughly with his hand. And then he started to sob, loudly. I was taken aback by his emotion. I'd never seen him anything other than happy or angry, so this was new, but at least sadness was a feeling I understood. "I fucking love you," he said through his choking sobs.

"I know. Please, Josh, look at the road. Why don't we pull over?"

"I said shut the fuck up! I fucking love you," he said again. I was so confused by this rollercoaster. Nothing made sense and nothing seemed to appease him, so I just sat quietly and closed my eyes, praying he would calm down and stop the car.

He took a deep, sharp breath and stopped crying, almost instantly.

"Let's get something straight," he said, wiping his face again. "*You* don't break up with *me*. *I'm* breaking up with *you*. I was going to break up with you anyway. I just wanted one last fuck around, and I knew you'd do it, you whore."

I kept my eyes closed, telling myself I would process these words later, but now I just wanted him to stop driving.

"Do you understand?" he barked. I nodded quickly. "Tell me you understand, or I will drive this fucking car into a tree. I swear to God, Andrea, I will kill myself and you. And nobody would give a shit. You remember that, okay? You are nothing, and if I have to fucking kill you, I will. And nobody would care."

My heart broke in my throat, and a wave of despair washed over my body. I felt as though I was suddenly on the outside, floating above myself, watching my body sit tensely in a speeding car next to a psychopath I had convinced myself I once loved. I let the tears stream out of my tired eyes. I couldn't hold them back anymore. I was so angry with myself for saying something. Didn't I know better? Had I learned nothing? He warned me so many times not to cross him, and here I was, crossing him in the biggest way. For a moment there, I'd thought I could win.

He jerked the car quickly, and I let out a scream.
He laughed.
"I understand!" I shouted. "I understand. You are

right, you broke up with me. I'm so sorry I ever thought otherwise." I just wanted this to be over.

He slammed on the brakes, pulling over to the shoulder of whatever highway we were on, the tires screeching so loudly that the noise imprinted itself in my mind. The car came to an abrupt stop. My body heaved forward against the seatbelt and then was shoved back into the seat from the force. Cars behind us started angrily honking as they drove past.

Josh unbuckled his seatbelt and grabbed my face with his hand, squeezing so hard that I felt my cheeks cave in.

"We're done," he said viciously, staring at me with such anger that my bones ached. "But you and me, Andie, we're never done." A malicious smile curled over his face. "So you go and do whatever it is you think you can do without me, but you better watch your fucking back." He let go of my face and leaned in close to me, his mouth so near my ear I could feel his hot breath. "You made a big mistake," he whispered softly, deliberately. He then moved his mouth to the base of my neck and started kissing me.

I shivered and let out a small whimper as I felt his chapped lips against my skin.

He lifted his head back up and looked at me, his eyes returning to their normal gaze, and he tilted his head as he wiped a tear from my face.

"Oh, sweetie," he said kindly. "Don't cry."

I didn't say anything. I was too scared to move. I just wanted to survive this moment, get back to school, and never see Josh again. But dread came over me as I realized we had a whole new school year coming up where we'd see each other every day. Maybe he'd lose interest over the summer. Maybe I'd tell my parents and confess that they were right, he wasn't a good guy. In fact, he was unstable. A lunatic. And they needed to protect me. Maybe we'd call the police. A thousand thoughts and scenarios ran through my mind as I sat there.

He finally pulled back and stroked my cheek with his finger.

"But you realize, if you tell anyone about this, or you try anything like this again, I *will* end us both. Okay?" He smiled. His cheery voice didn't match his horrible words. I nodded. "Good girl. Now let's get you back to school."

He turned on the car stereo, and "Because" by The Beatles began playing. I sat back in my seat, starting to process what had happened, and what this meant. I guess I *couldn't* tell my parents. Or anyone. I believed every syllable that came out of his unhinged mouth, especially when he said he would kill us both. He was just crazy enough to mean that. So I would have to just coast, looking over my shoulder all the while, until he tired of this and moved on. That is *if* he tired of this and moved on.

"Who's gonna want you now?" His words were pierced in my mind, I could hear them repeating over and over again. I reached into my pocket and turned my phone back on, looking down at the screen, shielding it from his view as he sang along to the music.

Carter: Too bad. Would've been nice to see you.

I deleted the message and bit my lip, unable to let any feelings from that text enter my atmosphere.

We drove in silence, accompanied by The Beatles until we got back to school. It was halfway through the third period when we arrived, and I didn't have the strength to fake that everything was okay or to wipe the trauma from my face before entering a classroom.

"I'm gonna go home," I said quietly.

Josh didn't respond, didn't look at me. He stepped out of the car, opened the trunk to grab his backpack, and started walking toward the school.

I walked slowly and carefully to my car in the parking lot and sat in the driver's seat. As I tried to back out, I glanced in my rearview mirror and thrust the car back into park after I saw my face, tear-stained and afraid. I buried my head in my hands, crying softly as the terror I had put aside to focus on survival started inching its way into my body now that I was safe. My only motivation throughout my relationship with Josh was purely to love and be loved. I couldn't understand why I was being so deeply punished for that?

My breath turned into choking gasps as I cried, alone in my car. Partially, I sobbed at the relief of freedom from no longer being tied to Josh in an official capacity since we were technically now broken up, and partially because of the gripping fear that reminded me I was not, and may never be, *truly* free of him. I also wept because I knew that he was right. Nobody would want me now.

Chapter Seventeen

When I finally calmed down enough to drive home, I texted my mom to let her know I wasn't feeling well and would be leaving school early. I steadied my hands and began driving. My phone rang immediately.

"Andrea? What's wrong?" My mom's worried voice echoed from the phone as I drove.

"Nothing, I just don't feel well." I tried to sound as normal as possible.

"Do you want me to come home?"

"No, no, I just want to lay down. It's fine. My English final isn't until tomorrow, so I'm not missing anything big. I'll probably feel better later. Sorry."

"Okay, well call me if you need anything. Feel better, sweetheart. I'll see you tonight."

I drove in silence with my thoughts. I wondered if Josh was telling anyone at school that we had broken up. Luckily, the semester was almost over, and summer break was approaching, which meant months of not having to see Josh every day. Maybe he would cool off over break, and things would go back to normal for our senior year.

But what did this mean for all the things we shared, like the band or our friendship with Harper? I shook my head and told myself the pieces would just fall where they may. If I had to quit the band, I would quit the band. Harper was leaving for college soon, so maybe that wouldn't be so hard. I just knew that I would not tell anybody about what happened today. I would let Josh decide the public narrative of our breakup, and I would calmly agree, feign sadness over the end of a relationship, and get through another year. He would forget me, as people so often did, and I could be invisible, which sounded so, so refreshing.

When I got home, I threw my backpack on the blue couch and retreated to my bedroom. Falling onto the unmade bed, I kicked my legs under the mess of sheets and blankets. I laid there, staring at the ceiling. No more tears fell. I had to focus. I had to survive. And if I shut up and played the part, if I pretended I missed Josh when someone asked, if I steered clear of his bad side and just remained timid and supportive, I could be okay. I vowed that I would never let myself feel as afraid again as I was in that car today. And if I let myself get immersed in the emotion of it, if I let myself fully feel the things that kept trying to creep in, I would fall apart.

My thoughts were interrupted by a chime from my phone. I picked it up to see a text from Ethan.

Ethan: I just heard—is it true?

Me: What did u hear?

I did not want to misstep depending on what story Josh was telling.

Ethan: Josh broke up with u— is it true?

Me: Yes.

I replied, not able to provide more detail.

Ethan: Whoa. You good?

I so badly wanted to say, to scream, "No, Ethan, I'm not good. I'm scared and broken, and I might be in danger. How are you?" Instead I settled with something safer.

Me: I'm okay.

Ethan: Want me to come over later?

And I really, really did, but I wasn't sure what the rules were yet. Was I allowed to talk to Ethan again? When Josh told me to watch my back, did he mean that he'd be checking up on me? And if I broke one of the rules he'd outlined during our relationship, would I be in trouble? Or had the rules changed?

"Thanks, but I'm okay." I decided to play it safe until I understood how to navigate these new waters better. Ethan's reaction made me feel a little better, though, knowing that I hadn't completely burned the bridge between us. Maybe he was aware that in light of recent events, what had kept me at arm's length lately was apparently no longer an issue. And God I hoped he was right. But it was too soon for me to know yet, so I had to be cautious.

Ethan: Ok. I'll check in later. Sorry, Andie, distance is a bitch.

Confused, I replied with a question mark.

Ethan: U and Josh—prob going to different colleges, so didn't make sense to stay together. Right? I get it. Makes sense. But still hard.

I let out a breath of relief. That was a good story, a straightforward story, that I could play along with. I felt grateful to Josh in that moment for telling it.

Me: Oh, yeah, it's tough, but I'll be okay.

I was unsure if that was true or not.

Ethan: Good thing *you* are tough, too ;)

I scoffed upon reading that. I wasn't tough. I wasn't strong. I was weak and scared. I always thought that was a secret I had to myself, but it was a secret I now shared with Josh. We both knew I was frail and unlovable. So Ethan's compliment felt like a mean joke. But I reminded myself that Ethan meant well. He didn't know my secret yet.

I stayed in bed for a few hours, trying to sleep, but mostly I just filled the time attempting to steer my mind away from worst-case scenarios and let myself enjoy the momentary stillness until my phone rang. It was Harper. I wasn't surprised.

"*What happened?*" she shouted into the phone when I answered. I couldn't tell if she was genuinely worried or if her panicked tone was exaggerated to cover up a smile.

"It's fine, it just ... wasn't going to work out. But I'm okay."

"Jesus, I did *not* see this coming. Are you upset?"

"Sure, but you know, it's high school. I guess I shouldn't have expected it to last forever." I tried my best to sound convincing and provide minimal detail so I wouldn't get confused.

"Wow, taking it like a champ," Harper said, which bothered me a little.

"What did Josh say?"

"Oh, um, not much." I could tell she was lying to make me feel better. It probably was better that I didn't know. "Just that it made sense to break up now before things got even more serious since he didn't want to do long distance during college."

"Yeah, that's about the sum of it."

"But you guys both seem to be taking it really well! So at least it's an easy breakup. I mean, that never happens, so at least there's that?" She really didn't have a clue.

"Yeah," I agreed, thinking of how I could change the subject. "Anyway, are you ready for prom this weekend? You still want me to come over and help you get ready?"

"Yes! That'd be great if you're up for it. I can't believe next week is my last week of high school."

"I know, I'm jealous." But she had no idea how jealous I really was that she was going to leave all of this behind her in a few short months.

"Andie, are you sure you're okay? You don't sound great," Harper said.

I wanted to tell her everything. I felt a strong pull to reach out and feel the comfort of my friend wrap around me and say it'd be okay. But I placed my hand over my mouth and shut my eyes tight, knowing it would only make things worse for everybody. I felt the fear bubble up again and I heard myself try to catch my breath, my mouth gasping behind my hand clasped tight over my lips to muffle my despair.

"Andie?" she asked again, growing more concerned.

I took a deep breath in through my nose and opened my eyes, placing my hand at my side.

"Yes, I'm okay." I steadied my voice and swallowed the panic, forcing myself back into the moment. "Did Josh seem okay?"

"Yeah ... I kinda hate to tell you this, but I saw him leave with Nicole and Lauren after school."

"From Kid A? Ugh, those vultures." I sighed. "The body's not even cold yet, and they're already swarming. Bitches."

"I know, right? Hopefully, he's not gonna fall down that rabbit hole, but they've taken down bigger prey before, so I won't hold my breath."

But then I realized, this might actually be the best-case scenario. If Josh immersed himself in the world of Kid A, he'd get just what he wanted, an adoring fan base, parties every weekend, all the sex and drugs a young wannabe rock star could dream of. I never thought I'd be grateful for Kid A, but I said a quick mental thank you to Nicole and Lauren for being just horrible and flashy enough to distract Josh when I needed him distracted the most.

"Yeah, well, it's been a weird day. I'm gonna just lay down for a while," I said. It felt good to talk to Harper like this again. I didn't realize how much I missed this during the Josh infiltration of our friendship. "But, Harper, thanks for calling. It means a lot."

"Um, duh! Sisters before misters." But I think we both knew how disingenuous that motto sounded now. I felt like I should apologize for my part, or explain. But instead, I just said my goodbyes and hung up. For the first time in a long time, I felt like I might actually miss Harper next year.

When my mom got home that evening, I heard her walk briskly to my room and then softly knock.

"Andrea, are you okay? How're you feeling?" she said as she entered.

"I'm feeling better, Mom. Don't worry. I'll be there for my final tomorrow."

"I'm not worried about that. I'm worried about you." She put her hand on my forehead and smiled when she realized there was no fever.

"Mom, I don't want to make a big deal out of this, but I figured you should probably know. Josh and I broke up today." I looked down at my hands.

"Oh my gosh, Andrea. I'm sorry, honey. Are you all right? What happened?" She sounded concerned and relieved at the same time.

"I don't really want to talk about it. But yes, I'm all right."

I wanted just to get the facts out and move on so she couldn't catch me in a lie or sense my deceit when I had to tell the fake story.

She sat down on my bed and embraced me tightly.

I reached around to complete the hug and closed my eyes as I felt the emotions start peeking through again. *Don't do it*, I silently told myself, knowing that my mom was always able to get me to talk about things when I didn't want to. And I couldn't tell her what happened. Josh would view that as a betrayal, and I believed every hate-filled word of his threats, so I swallowed and breathed and reminded myself of the seriousness of the situation so I could get a clearer head.

She pulled back from the hug. "I'm here if you want to talk."

"I know, thanks."

My phone chimed, and I grabbed it, nervous it was Josh but sighed when I saw it was Ethan.

"I'm going to start dinner," my mom said. "Come down when you're ready."

I nodded, checking my phone.

She stood up and headed toward the stairs, giving me a final smile as she exited.

Ethan: U should come to my show now. That will make u feel better. Carter asked me if u were coming. Sup with that? ;)

I wanted to go. I really wanted to go. I owed it to Ethan to support him in this exciting debut, and any day I got to have eyes on Carter was a good day, even if it meant I'd have to see Sloane hanging on him. But I was nervous that Josh would find out and somehow, for some reason, invent a way to be angry about it. I wondered if I should ask his permission. But that wouldn't help. Even if he said yes, he could always change his mind and say I should've figured it out. And I couldn't just assume he wouldn't find out, for all I knew he would be there, too. Kid A was typically a staple at Intentionally Blank shows. And even if he wasn't there, he seemed to always know where I was and who I was with, so evasion was pointless. But then my mind went to Harper. She was the perfect shield. Josh gushed over Harper. He'd never be mad if I were just tagging along with her.

Before I responded to Ethan, I quickly shot a text to Harper.

Me: Hey, I was thinking, I'd prob feel better if I got out of the house. Want to go to the Blank show together on Sunday?

I anxiously waited for her to reply, tapping my fingers together to help time pass quickly. Finally, my phone buzzed.

Harper: Ya! Prom is Sat and show on Sun—busy weekend! I'm in.

I opened Ethan's message and replied.

Me: Ok! Harper and I will be there.

I felt an instant relief. I had a plan. And I had something to look forward to. If anything, watching Carter perform would just give me more ammo for my daydream fantasies. And this would help solidify my hopefully on-the-mend friendship with Ethan, too. And if Josh were there, I would be armed with Harper to diffuse any tension. I was ready.

Chapter Eighteen

By the time Sunday evening rolled around, I was shocked that I hadn't heard a word from Josh since the breakup. He had completely ignored me at rehearsal on Friday and hadn't texted me at all. For the first time in months, I had some breathing room, but I knew better than to let my guard down completely. If my relationship with Josh had taught me anything, it was that I could plan for nothing. I had to just prepare myself for constant surprise and learn how to roll with the unpredictable.

In every conversation I had with Ethan, I could feel Josh's breath on the back of my neck, even when he was nowhere to be seen. And when Stephanie heard the news and told me she always knew Josh was bad news, I defended him, telling her that he was just misunderstood and had been a great boyfriend, just because I felt like he was right there next to me, coaxing the words out of my body, even if he was invisible. But I still enjoyed the new artificial freedom I had, even if it *was* sheltered and heavily monitored.

I had finished most of my final exams and next week was the last week of the school year. There was a buzz in the halls about our breakup, but not as much as I had expected. There was more talk about Josh's head-first dive into the world of Kid A and rumors about him getting caught smoking pot with Lauren and Nicole. I didn't know if it was true, but I didn't doubt it either. I hoped it was true. That would mean that Josh was busy. Honestly, Kid A was much more his speed than I ever was. He was probably thrilled.

When I saw Harper's car pull into the driveway, I ran outside and hopped in the passenger seat.

"Okay, start from the beginning," I said excitedly,

pushing her to give me all the details about prom, which was the night before.

She smiled. "It was fun," she said as she started driving.

"That's it? 'It was fun?' Come on. You gotta give me more than that."

"No, I mean, it was cool. Brandon was chill, but honestly, we didn't even spend *that* much time together, which was kinda weird. He kinda clung to his friends once we got there and, I don't know, the whole thing was sorta cheesy." She shrugged.

"Oh, so then what?"

"Well, don't be mad, but Nicole had a party afterward, and I didn't expect to be invited. I was just gonna go home, but Josh texted me and said I should come, so I went. It wasn't a big deal, just some annoying Kid A bitches and a few guys I didn't know."

"And Josh," I said bluntly, making sure she knew I had heard that part.

"Yeah, don't be mad. Honestly, it wasn't even that fun." She was talking quickly and in a higher pitch that normal.

"I'm not mad, Harp, you can hang out with whoever you want.

I didn't know how to feel about this news. My gut reaction was to be annoyed. I hated that Josh had this great, fun life without me. Naively I guess I had hoped he'd miss me and be devastated with me out of his life, but if anything, it sounded like he was happier and having a blast. Logic reminded me that if Josh stayed fixated on me, that was a *bad* thing, a dangerous thing, and I should be grateful. But I couldn't shake the nagging feeling of wanting to be missed, wanting to be desired.

"Sorry it wasn't as fun as you had hoped," I said, thinking she was probably lying about her enjoyment to soften the blow of telling me she was not only hanging out with our sworn enemies but also my ex-boyfriend. I pushed the annoyance out of my head and tried to focus on the night ahead. I had been excited about this for days, and I didn't want to ruin it before it even started, so I changed the subject.

"Tonight should be fun though, yeah?" I asked.

"Yeah! I'm stoked," Harper replied. "I mean, the guys from Intentionally Blank better get used to seeing me in the crowd since I'll be at every U of M show next year."

"Ugh, you're so lucky." I sunk back in my seat slightly as my mind faded back to Josh while Harper droned on about the decor plans for her dorm room as she drove. When we pulled up to the venue, which was an intimate theater that doubled as a concert hall on the weekends, I snapped back into the moment.

"I hope we're not late," she said as we parked. I smoothed out my skirt and double checked my makeup in the side mirror before stepping out of the car. I felt nervous, but not in the way I had been lately. It was more of a fun nervous, with flecks of anticipatory excitement. I smiled at Harper. We looked like an odd pair, her in frumpy purple corduroys and a baggy knitted sweater, and me in a snug red skirt with black tights and a denim jacket over my snow leopard print blouse (which took many outfit changes to finally select).

When we got inside, it was already packed, so we had to elbow our way to the front row. Luckily the band hadn't started yet. I looked around and saw a lot of familiar faces. It felt like the entire school was there. But the guys from Intentionally Blank were our small town's version of celebrities, so it wasn't unexpected. I motioned to a small gathering of Kid A near the back and made a gagging noise to Harper, which she returned, giggling, until one of them waved at Harper, trying to catch her attention. I think her name was Alexis. She was always hanging around Nicole, and I recognized her from the nose ring and thick eyeliner.

Harper gave a quick wave and turned around, her face turning red.

"She was at Nicole's last night," she said sheepishly. "But trust me, she's just as annoying as you'd expect. She got drunk and started singing Taylor Swift songs. Taylor Swift! Even though she was wearing a Taking Back Sunday sweatshirt. She's *so* fake."

"Ha," I said, trying not to let any of this bother me. Luckily, the lights dimmed at that moment, and the band walked out. I loudly cheered when I saw Ethan take his seat behind the drums. He looked confident, prepared. Carter walked out last, and I felt my stomach flip when I saw him. His charcoal slacks and blue jersey cotton Karma Police t-shirt hung on his sculpted body effortlessly, and his long dark hair was pulled back with a few wisps falling near his face.

"We are Intentionally Blank!" he shouted into the microphone as the audience cheered. "Thanks for coming out on this Sunday night. We're stoked to play the first live show with our new drummer, Mr. Ethan Marks," he said, pointing toward the drum set, as Ethan gave a short wave with the sticks in his hand. "Let's go!" Carter yelled, now pointing to the crowd, and the band dove into their first song.

Harper and I felt the crowd pushing against us since we were at the front, so she pushed back and carved out a tiny circle for herself on the floor as she started dancing wildly, her eyes closed and hands swinging. Her carefree attitude was infectious, and I wanted to join her, but I couldn't shake the feeling that I'd look ridiculous, so I stuck with swaying and moving my feet to the beat, singing as loud as I could when I knew the words.

They sounded good. Really, really good. Carter's voice was flawless, his falsetto gave me goosebumps, and his energy bled into the crowd. I turned toward the back of the venue, and that's when I saw Josh, out of the corner of my eye at first, and then all at once as I focused on him while he stood by Alexis and now Nicole, our eyes locking.

He nodded toward me and then pointed at Harper, who was still flailing on the dance floor and laughed, shooting me a thumbs up.

I smiled and turned back around quickly, feeling the people behind me pushing up against my back as I stood there, trying to decipher what had happened. Did he think we were friends? Could we be friends? Wasn't he mad? I knew Harper was a good safety net, but I never expected Josh and I would have a *friendly* interaction. I thought best-case scenario would be him ignoring me.

After a few more songs, Harper had finally spotted Josh, too, and waved obnoxiously in his direction. He whispered something in Nicole's ear and then started making his way toward us.

I froze, and the person behind me saw an advantage when I stopped swaying and shoved himself in front of me. I started sinking back into the crowd as people pushed past me. Suddenly I felt a familiar hand creep its way around my waist and I closed my eyes, knowing Josh had found me.

"Hey, sexy," he crooned, his breath reeking of alcohol.

"Are you drunk?" I asked, instantly wishing I hadn't. I didn't want him to think I was being judgmental, but I'd never seen him like this.

"You looking good tonight, baby," he shouted

over the music as he brushed my hair off my shoulder and kissed it sloppily. I shot my gaze toward the stage and caught eyes quickly with Carter. I hated that he saw me with Josh, but I loved that he saw me.

I didn't stop Josh. I knew better. I just stood there, trying to catch Harper's eye. When she finally found me in the crowd, I tried to flash her a panicked look, and she got the hint, squeezing her way through the crowd to meet us.

"What's up, Josh!" she said as she approached.

"I'm gonna run to the bathroom," I said, excusing myself and disappearing behind the sea of people as Harper distracted him.

When I got into a stall, I locked the door and buried my hands in my face, trying to calm down as I felt my body shake. A visceral fear pulsed through my veins and the tension hung so thick I thought I would choke before I ever caught my breath. Even in the middle of so many people, I wasn't safe. Josh could do whatever he wanted to me, we both knew that already, but the truly crushing realization came in that moment when I knew I would let him. And I hated myself for that.

I asked myself why I got so dressed up. Yes, I had wanted Carter to see me looking nice, but not at the risk of unwelcome hands and lips brushing against me in a busy crowd. I shuddered as I recalled the feeling. And I should know by now that it didn't matter if I looked the best I possibly could, it would never be good enough for someone like Carter. I shook my head and tried to push the skin-crawling discomfort out of my body as I exited the stall, planning to splash some water on my face and reenter the event until the door came swinging open as Sloane entered, an unlit cigarette hanging out of her mouth.

"Oh shit, sorry, didn't think anyone would be in

here during the show," she said, sounding annoyed. "You mind?" She lifted a lighter out of her purse.

"No," I said softly. I had never talked to Sloane before, but I felt instantly awkward as if she somehow knew how many times I'd wished to be her, to have her comfortable life.

"Thanks." She flicked the lighter to the end of the cigarette and took a deep inhale. "Can I ... help you?" she asked rudely. Apparently, I was staring.

"Oh, sorry." I quickly looked at the ground. She was so pretty. I hated it. "Hey, aren't you dating Carter Wells?" I asked, already knowing the answer.

"Yeah ... what are you, like, stalking me?" She scoffed and let out a sarcastic laugh. I pursed my lips, not knowing what to say. I could've, and probably should've, just left after she walked in, but I needed to talk to her. I thought if I were close to her, I could understand what Carter saw in her, and maybe in a weird way it'd make me feel better.

"No, sorry, I just, I know him a little bit. Well, I know Ethan. Ethan Marks. The new drummer." I was stammering.

"Yeah, I know who Ethan is..." This was not going well.

"Right, cool, I mean, of course," I continued, even though my mind was telling me in no uncertain terms to stop.

Sloane turned away from me and opened the bathroom window a crack to flick her cigarette out.

I wasn't satisfied yet. I wanted to press more. Carter wasn't just gorgeous, he also seemed passionate and engaging and remarkably friendly. Sloane, from what I could tell so far, was just gorgeous.

"They sound good tonight, huh?" I asked, hoping to engage her further.

"Honestly, I've been to so many shows, they all kinda sound the same. At least I'll get a break this summer."

I appreciated this for two reasons. First, she was talking to me now like a real person, and second, it sounded like she might not be around this summer, which meant there was a slightly greater possibility I could see Carter without her leering over his shoulder.

"Oh? What's this summer?" I asked, trying not to sound excited.

"I'm studying abroad in Italy for a few months." She took a long drag of her cigarette.

"Wow, that's really cool. I'm Andrea, by the way."

"Sloane," she said, eyeing me up and down, her long, manicured lashes fluttering. "How did you say you know Carter again?"

"I don't really. I mean just a little bit through friends. I'm Ethan's friend." The sound of the song coming from the venue changed to a slower tune, one I didn't recognize. "Is this new?" I asked, pointing toward the door from where the sound was coming.

"Oh, yeah, I think this is some new piece Carter was working on. I don't really keep track anymore. I'm a little bored with the whole fangirl scene. I mean, I get it, he's good and all, but Jesus." She rolled her hazel eyes. Looking in the mirror, she adjusted the silver leather band that twisted through her thick braid which started dark at the roots and fell into a light blonde ombre through the ends.

"I'm gonna go check out the new song," I said, backing toward the door.

"Of course you are, hon." She didn't take her eyes away from the mirror. I was right to hate her all along. She was awful. And it made their whole relationship feel so unjust. But I understood. It was the same old story I'd grown to expect. She may be an uninspiring snob at heart, but you couldn't tear your eyes away from her. No wonder she got along so well with Nicole. I had always thought, or dreamed I guess, that Carter could see through that, that he was above it. But my suspected fears were right all along. Nobody was immune from Kid A.

As I made my way back into the audience, I heard unfamiliar, clunky chords being passionately pounded out on a piano from the stage. I tried to insert myself into the middle of the crowd so as to avoid Josh and Harper picking me out. Carter was on the stage by himself, sitting behind a piano, in the middle of an apparently new song. Some of his loose hair was sticking to the sweat glistening on his chiseled face while other wisps bounced rhythmically as his head banged along with the keys as he played. He wasn't a particularly technical or skilled pianist, but goddamn he sounded good.

"And if you can love a piano man/baby I can be your piano man," he sang, slowly and brilliantly, with his eyes closed as he hung on every note. "Was it a memory or a dream/when I held you so close/you don't know how beautiful you are." I was mesmerized. It felt like I was suddenly alone in a crowded room, completely entranced by his melody, his intensity. "I would love you like he can't love you/I would kiss you in slow motion/I could be your piano man, baby/just let me play you a song." He held the last word for several long seconds before lightly letting his fingers off the keys and opening his eyes. The crowd erupted in cheers, and he let out his signature half smile. "Thank you. Thanks, everyone," he said humbly on the microphone. "Just a new one I'm trying out, so thanks for humoring me. All right, since you so kindly let me get all serious for a sec, let's bring the band back out, and we'll give you the good ole' fashioned rock you came here to see!" More cheers came as Ethan and the others walked back out, taking their places on stage before starting up again.

Still transfixed from the last song, I couldn't get it out of my mind. The melody was haunting, his voice enchanting. And then I saw Sloane slip out of the bathroom and walk toward the back, sitting at a high-top table with Nicole, looking unamused. I was so angry that she would get to leave this show with the same man that just left his heart on the stage, and she had barely even noticed.

Before I could let my thoughts take me too far down this path, I heard Harper's voice call my name over the loud music.

I finally spotted her a few feet away and pushed past some people to get to her.

"Hey, sorry, I was in the bathroom," I said.

"No worries, but hey I gotta jet. Josh is wasted, and Nicole is refusing to drive him home. She's afraid he's going to puke in her new car. Ugh, she's really the worst," Harper said hurriedly. "I'm really sorry. I hate to leave you, but you can get a ride home with Ethan, right?"

"Yeah, okay." I was half furious at her for leaving me for Josh and half thrilled that it meant Josh would be leaving.

"I'll make it up to you, I promise."

"Go," I said, motioning toward Josh in the back, who was already stumbling toward the door.

"I owe you, Andie," Harper said as she jogged to catch him before he staggered outside. When they were gone, I hung toward the back of the crowd for the rest of the concert, feeling a little out of place by myself.

After the encore, Carter thanked the audience for

a great show, and the band went backstage as the lights came up. Everyone started talking and milling toward the exits while I pressed my way upstream to try and get Ethan's attention.

When I finally made it to the front, I darted through a hallway that seemed to lead backstage and squeezed by several people and large pieces of sound equipment until I saw Ethan's drum set, partially taken apart. I figured he was taking it out to his car in pieces, so I waited near it until I saw him come back.

"Ethan!" I waved at him.

"Andie! You made it!" he shouted, giving me a big hug.

"You were incredible! You killed it. I'm so proud of you."

"Thanks! It means a lot that you came. Are you here with Harper?"

"Yeah, but she had to split early." I didn't want to explain further. "Can a girl get a ride from her famous drummer friend?" I smiled.

"Ha, of course, I'm almost done here. Want to grab a cymbal and bring it outside for me? My car's out back."

"Sure." I unscrewed his crash cymbal from its stand. As I walked through the large open door leading to Ethan's parked car in the back lot, I shivered in the chilly spring air and tried to find a free space in his trunk quickly.

"Andrea."

I heard a familiar voice call from behind me. It was Carter. I turned around and smiled, feeling crippled by nerves and yet lifted by enthusiasm.

"You made it," he said through that goddamn half smile.

"Yes, I made it. You were ... you are ... you

135

sounded so good." I tried to choose my words carefully and poetically but ended up flustered instead, per usual.

"Thanks, I had hoped you'd be here."

"*You did*?" I didn't mean to sound as shocked as I was. "I mean, honestly, Carter, you are so damn talented. And your new song, wow. I've never seen you solo like that. Fucking stunning." I instantly questioned myself. Should I not have sworn? Was it too gruff? Or did it give me some much-needed credibility? Was I complimenting him too much? Not enough? I decided to stop talking.

"Yeah? You liked it?"

"Liked it? I loved it. Really, really great stuff."

"Excuse me, bozos," Ethan said as he approached with his snare drum, placing it in the trunk and then slipping back inside for another load. "Andie, these drums aren't gonna load themselves!" he shouted behind him, half joking.

"Coming!" I said. "I'd better..."

"Haha, yeah yeah, he plays one show with us, and he's already calling the shots." Carter laughed. "Anyway, who are you here with? Where's your piano man?" His dark eyes sparkled as he stared intently at me.

"My piano man? Josh?" I asked, confused until suddenly I connected the dots. Was he ... no, I couldn't let my mind go there. "We're not together anymore. As of last week."

"Well, that's a loss for the piano man then." Carter's eyes never left mine as he spoke. I couldn't breathe. Was his song ... no, I had to stop thinking like that. I couldn't get my hopes up.

Sloane came bursting through the back door.

"Carter, come on, you said we could leave like ten minutes ago. Oh, hi fangirl," she said when she saw me.

"Sloane, this is Andrea," he said politely, his eyes

glued to me the whole time, making every inch of my body feel like it might explode.

"Yeah, well, excuse me fangirl, but Mr. Wells has left the building," she said rudely. "Come on, Carter," she persisted, grabbing his arm.

I would've done anything at that moment to know what his arm felt like.

"I'll see you around ... Andie," he said, keeping his gaze on me as he walked backward a few steps, smiled, and turned around to follow Sloane. I gasped to catch my breath when he was out of sight and felt my face flush with heat.

"Alright, this is the last one," Ethan announced as he dragged out another drum stand and tossed it in the back seat. "You ready?"

"Yes," I said, still looking in the direction that Carter disappeared. "Let's go."

Chapter Nineteen

The week after the concert, I could barely concentrate. I couldn't stop thinking about Carter and his song. I hadn't heard anything from him, but I didn't really expect to. I wouldn't allow myself to be set up for embarrassment by assuming Carter had even a minuscule amount of feelings for me. *Maybe* we shared a moment that night in the alley behind the theater, but it was fleeting, and he left with Sloane. Those were the facts that I reminded myself over and over again when my thoughts would start floating to something that resembled hope.

It was the last week of the school year, and luckily Josh had ignored me in the halls since his drunken approach at the concert. The rumors continued swirling about him getting involved in darker substances with Kid A, and I even heard that several people assumed that was why we broke up. It was no secret how straight edge I was, and for the first time, I didn't mind since it publicly drew a thicker dividing line between Josh and me.

When the last bell rang on the final day of school, everyone cheered and sprinted through the halls, but I walked calmly to pack up my locker. I was happy to be out of school but nervous about what the summer would entail. At least at school I saw Josh in a controlled environment, but with summer came spontaneity, and that terrified me.

I knew my dad wanted me to find a summer job, and the more I thought about it, the more that seemed like a good idea. It would help make the free days a little more structured and predictable, so I decided I'd start applying that weekend. But over dinner that night, my dad had a surprise announcement.

"Andrea, I've got great news," he exclaimed, seemingly quite proud of himself. "I know today was your last day of school, so I talked to Roger at the club, and he'd love to have you take the afternoon shift at the clubhouse this summer!"

Roger Jansen was the general manager at the local country club, of which my parents were active members.

"The clubhouse?" I asked, nervously. The clubhouse was a little hut that sat against the golf course, offering drinks and snacks to golfers at the ninth hole. I knew the girl who worked the evening shift, Rebecca, from school. We were in English class together, and she always bragged about her job. Apparently, the tips were great, and you got to be in the clubhouse by yourself during your shift, so she'd spend her downtime watching videos on her phone and finishing homework. She made it sound like the easiest job ever, so my anxiety didn't come from the prospect of the job. It seemed like a pretty sweet setup. But the clubhouse sat directly across the street from Josh's house. So he'd know exactly where I was during my shifts, and I'd be alone in between customers. This whole idea completely negated my intention for the summer.

"I don't know, Dad. I think I'll apply to a couple of other places before I make up my mind."

"Don't be crazy! I already told Roger you'd take it. I thought you'd be thrilled! Your friends would probably kill for this job. Think how much you'll make in tips alone. You'll be all set when it comes time for dorm shopping."

He didn't get it. He couldn't get it. And I didn't know how to explain my fears.

"I just ... I'm going to look at a couple of other

options," I started, but he interrupted me.

"Andrea, come on now, I did you a huge favor here. You start a week from Monday. Roger is going to send you the details this weekend. I thought you'd be jumping for joy!"

"No, Dad, you're right, I'm sorry. Thank you."

I was stuck. And I had a week to prepare. Maybe Josh wouldn't find out? But I knew that was impossible. I'd surely see his parents at least, and they would tell him. Somebody would tell him.

I gave Harper the news that night on the phone.

"Shut *up*!" she said. "You're *so* lucky. You basically will get paid a shitload of money to sit on your ass and serve overpriced crap to drunk rich people. Jackpot!"

"Yeah," I said, trying to mask my concerns.

"Well, we have two months until I move to Ann Arbor for school, so let's make this summer count."

"Of course," I agreed. "It'll be great."

I tried to enjoy the next week before I started my new job. I went shopping with Harper, watched old movies with Ethan, and spent one unusually hot day with Stephanie at her aunt's backyard pool. There was no word from Josh, even Harper didn't mention him when we hung out. It was almost as if he didn't exist. By the weekend, I wasn't even looking over my shoulder when I left my house. But my newfound peace was quickly interrupted when my phone chimed. I looked down to see a message from Josh.

Josh: Hi.

I hated the one-word text. It was open to so many interpretations. I didn't know if he was trying to start a conversation or if he had something important to tell me, or if it was something else entirely, but I didn't want any of it. Even if he was reaching out to apologize, I didn't want to know. I had loved the freedom that a life without Josh had offered me this past week.

I wrote back quickly, knowing I had no choice but to respond.

Me: Hi.

After a few minutes, his next text came in.

Josh: Clubhouse?

Me: Yes.

I knew he would find out. It had only been a matter of time. I wondered what he was doing. Was he at home? Was he with Nicole? Was he high? Drunk? What had made him think of me right then? He didn't reply, and the silence filled the room. I kept checking my phone in case I had missed the sound, but I hadn't. And then an eerie feeling washed over me as I realized that he had just wanted me to know that he knew. That he knew where I would be, what I'd be doing, and what kind of power that knowledge gave him.

I suddenly felt like I was back in that car, speeding into an unknown fate with a taunting psychopath at the wheel. My hands shook, so I curled my fingers into fists to force them into stillness. I exhaled the breath I had unknowingly been holding and told myself it would be okay, even though I knew better. I just had to get through each day until the summer was over, and then until the next school year was over, and then one more summer, and I'd be gone. I couldn't think of the time in one large chunk of days, or it would overwhelm me at best, so I'd just get through each day as it came.

By the time Monday rolled around, I had readied myself for the first day of work, putting my hair in a tight bun and dressing in an oversized polo shirt. I didn't wear any makeup, and I found an unflattering pair of khakis in my mom's closet that were way too big. I had decided that anytime I knew I could have a reasonable chance of running into Josh, I wouldn't let myself wear anything that even mildly hugged my body. My goal was to look as much like an invisible blob as possible.

Josh hated when I wore my hair up, so I would wear my hair up. Josh had made many aggressively sexual comments about my body as I got thinner and thinner, and since I was still having trouble keeping food down, I would invest in baggy clothes to hide my shrinking frame. If I didn't tempt him, he wouldn't want me, and if he didn't want me, he wouldn't hurt me. It was logical, and I was proud of my new plan. I never felt attractive in my normal life, but I knew there was something about me and my body that resonated with Josh's desires, so I would exploit that. There was safety in being invisible, in being unattractive, and that's how I would get myself through each day.

When I arrived at the clubhouse, I could see Josh's car in his driveway across the street, which immediately gave me an uneasy feeling. I tried to ignore it and press on, parking in the employee lot and walking over to the cramped hut amidst the lush golf course, trying to quickly walk as it felt like he was watching me, even though I didn't see him. When I entered the clubhouse, I let out a sigh of relief when I saw Roger.

"Hi, Andrea," he said happily. "I was just getting things set up here for you. Rebecca will be training you. You guys know each other, right?"

"A little bit, from school."

"Great. She'll be with you for the first week until you get the hang of things and then you'll be on your own. Think you can handle it?"

"Yes, of course." My eyes darted from the front window to the back window, scanning the surroundings.

"Great. I grabbed your uniform from the main building," he said, holding up some folded black fabric.

"Uniform?" I asked, swallowing my anxiety.

"Yeah, all the employees here wear black polos with the club logo. I've got a couple here for you to choose from. What do you wear? Small?"

I had never been small in my life. Had I lost *that* much weight? I didn't know whether to feel proud or disgusted.

"Do you have an extra-large?" I asked, praying he would let me keep up my new strategy.

"We do ... but I must remind you that one of our pillars here is professionalism, and that includes employee appearance, so I'd prefer you wear something fitted. Comfortable of course, but fitted."

I hung my head down. I would have to make this work, but at least I could keep up *some* of my new routine. I'd keep my hair tied back, I wouldn't wear makeup, and I'd seek out the most unflattering pants I could find.

"I'll take a medium."

"Wonderful, there's a bathroom behind the clubhouse where you can change. Rebecca should be here any minute, and I'll leave you girls to it. I left your new hire paperwork in the front office so just make sure to stop in there today. Happy to have you aboard!" He handed me a name tag.

I thanked him for the opportunity and retreated to the bathroom. As I slipped on the scratchy new polo and smoothed out the creases, I looked in the mirror and hated every thread of the fabric that touched my skin, making me less invisible. You could see the outline of my breasts and my waist as the shirt clung to my body, making me appear prettier than I knew I really was. I pulled on the ends of the top, trying to stretch out the fabric to make it less form fitting. I wanted it to be as straight as possible, but after a few attempts to extend it,

Rebecca walked in.

"Hi. Andrea, right? We had English together?"

"Yeah, that's right," I replied, pretending to have just been smoothing over my shirt.

"Cool! Happy to meet you officially. You'll love this job. It's cake. You ready to get started?"

Chapter Twenty

The job *was* easy. And the tips *were* great. Rebecca had been right about that. But every day that I came to work, I wondered if that would be the day that Josh would stop by and make himself known. After a couple of weeks went by, he still hadn't appeared. His car was there most days, but even on days it wasn't, I expected to see it drive by at any time.

One day, after my shift ended, I was walking to my car in the parking lot and quickly stopped when I saw Josh leaning up against it.

"Hey, you," he said with a cordial smile as if that were perfectly normal.

I tried to smile back but the alarms in my body were going off so loudly I don't know if I actually did. I took a deep breath and tried to calm my racing thoughts that were quickly plotting escape plans.

"I gotta say, it's pretty nice having you so close all day. Much easier to keep track of you this way than it was when I had to actually drive by your house."

I closed my eyes as the nausea started to take over. He had been following me, checking on me. I shouldn't have been surprised, but I was. I had really hoped that maybe things were resolving on their own. But I should've known better. He was unstable, unpredictable, and seemingly obsessed. That didn't just go away on its own.

"What? Not going to say hi?" he asked.

"Hi."

He started to walk toward me, and my eyes darted to see who else was around, but it was eerily quiet.

"I've missed you. I think about you ... a lot. Your skin, your body." He got uncomfortably close and grabbed one of my breasts over the scratchy polo as he kissed my jaw.

I finally saw an older couple walking to their car, probably having come from the restaurant. I tried to shoot them a look of panic, but they continued to mind their own business as they got into their Cadillac.

His breath was hot and reeked of smoke. "Just because we're not together, don't think that means that the rules don't still apply," he whispered in my ear as his hand moved to my waist.

I closed my eyes, feeling the fear take over and the autopilot click on.

He put his hands by his side and took a couple of steps back, tilting his head and looking through me with a piercing stare. "Don't worry, Andie. You've always been a good girl. I'm sure you'll be okay. Look, I don't *want* to hurt you. Or myself, for that matter. I just will *have* to if it comes to that. But you know that. We've already had this conversation. I think sometimes it just helps to have a friendly reminder."

A big, authentic smile came over his face. I didn't know how to talk to him anymore. I couldn't guess what he wanted me to say, so I just nodded. At this point, nobody would believe me even I did tell.

"I'll see you later, okay, beautiful?" He leaned in and kissed my cheek before turning and heading toward his house.

I was shaken and disgusted. I didn't know what to do. Josh had me up against a wall. He knew it, and I knew it. I just had to watch my step and get through each day. I couldn't let the feelings bubble up because they would consume me. And being emotional, not thinking straight, could be the difference between life and death. So I would just exist until I didn't anymore.

Another week went by, and I hadn't seen or heard

from Josh. The relief was only minimal, though, because I still felt him everywhere.

One day I showed up to work and noticed the skies turning dark gray.

"Great," I muttered to myself sarcastically. Rainy days were the most boring because nobody golfed in the rain, but I still had to sit there and pass the time, with no tips coming in. As I settled in for a long shift, I opened my phone to search for a distraction and almost dropped it when it started ringing. Carter's name popped up on the caller ID, and I threw my phone onto the counter in front of me, as if it had suddenly grown spikes. I couldn't answer it, what would I say? And why was he calling? Why didn't he just text me if he wanted to talk? I stared at my phone as it rang until it finally stopped.

One missed call—Carter Wells. The phone mocking me from the wooden countertop. I stayed silent and held my breath, anxiously wondering if he would leave a message. I resounded to the idea that maybe he called me by accident. The voicemail chime rang out, and I exhaled, grabbing my phone and putting it to my ear as the voicemail played.

"Hey, Andrea, it's Carter Wells. Long time no talk. Wanted to see what you were up to tonight? I was going to have Ethan and a few others over to the loft to hang out. Would love to see you there. Call me back, K? Take care."

I set my phone down, bewildered. My first loft party. I *had* to go. I picked up the phone again and opened a text to Harper but then stopped myself. I didn't want to share this with her. I didn't want to risk it getting back to Josh, and I felt like Harper would somehow ruin this. I felt guilty thinking that, but something just didn't feel right about it, so I texted Stephanie instead.

Me: Steph! Just got a call from *Carter Wells*

inviting me to loft party 2night. WTF???

She responded within a minute.

Stephanie: You're on fire, girrrrrrl, now that you got that loser out of your life. Go for it! Duh!! Have fun, use protection, and call me 2morrow!"

Me: Shut up!!

She was always so dramatic.

Me: What do I do about curfew?

I knew she'd have the answer.

Stephanie: What do you mean? You're staying at my house tonight, right? ;)

I hadn't even considered lying to my parents. I'd never done that before. Would it work? I could tell them I was staying at Stephanie's, go to the loft party, and then *actually* sneak into Steph's afterward to sleep. It was common knowledge that Stephanie didn't have a curfew. She was the youngest of six and the only one of her siblings who still lived at home. After having raised five other kids successfully, her parents were famously laidback about her whereabouts. My parents, on the other hand, cared a lot. I didn't think I could lie to them. But then I remembered how much I *hadn't* told them lately, how much I had kept from them about Josh's behavior, the threats, my fears. And then I thought about Carter and how every part of me wanted to see him tonight. To be his personally invited guest. To see him in his element. So I texted my mom.

Me: Okay if I hang out with Stephanie tonight and sleep over?

I bit my lip as I waited for her response. I felt like she would somehow know I was lying.

Mom: Sure—have fun! And don't be home too late tomorrow morning since you still have to work.

I couldn't believe it.

Me: Thanks, love you!

I replied and then quickly wrote to Stephanie.

Me: You are the best.

She responded with a heart emoji.

It was settled. I was going to my first loft party. I had dreamed of this ever since I first laid eyes on Carter and heard about these mysterious gatherings. But I had always just resigned myself to the fact that I would explore the world of parties in college, and until then, my most raucous nights would involve Diet Coke, Twizzlers, and maybe, if we were lucky, an R-rated movie in Harper's basement. Then I met Josh, and I escalated my rebellious expectations to include the occasional make-out session. But an actual party had never even entered my mind. Not just because I'd never been invited, which I hadn't, but also because I'd always assumed I wouldn't be allowed to go, which I wouldn't. So I wrote off the idea. But now I was not only going to a party, I was going to a loft party, at the personal request of Carter Wells. I couldn't wipe the smile off my face. I couldn't call Carter back without sounding like a grinning idiot, so I sent him a simple text.

Me: Got your message—I'll be there, thanks for inviting. I'll get w/ Ethan for details.

He sent back a smiley face, and I let out an audible squeal as I hurriedly tapped out a message to Ethan to secure plans.

The already boring day at work seemed to drag on endlessly as I cataloged outfits and conversation topics in my head, preparing for my night. I hoped, prayed, that Sloane was already in Italy so she wouldn't be there to throw a wet blanket of eye-rolling and Carter-hogging on the evening.

When Rebecca finally showed up to relieve me from my shift, I practically ran to my car. I couldn't wait to start getting ready. I knew Josh wouldn't be there, so I had no concerns with looking my best for one night, and after weeks of starched khakis and greasy pulled-back hair, the thought of curling mascara and a high-heat hair straightener actually excited me.

As I made my way to the car, I instinctively looked toward Josh's house and saw a familiar junky white hatchback in the driveway and stopped in my tracks. It was Harper's car.

"Ugh," I said under my breath. Of *course,* they were hanging out. And of course, she wouldn't mention it to me the next time we talked. I filed this information in the back of my head, telling myself I would revisit it tomorrow when I had the time to focus on it. Right now, I had to get ready for a loft party.

Chapter Twenty-One

"Wow," Ethan said as I stepped out of my car into his driveway. I'd met him at his house so we could drive to Carter's loft together. "I don't usually think this kind of thing about you, no offense, but you look ... really nice," he said, his eyes widening.

"Shut up." I responded playfully, secretly loving his comments. If Ethan, who was like my brother, thought I looked nice, that must mean I really do. After a lot of back-and-forths, I had finally settled on wearing a teal v-neck cotton summer dress with a dark denim jacket and knee-high boots. I wore my hair in soft, beachy waves and applied rose-colored eyeshadow with matching lip gloss. For the first time in as long as I could remember, I felt pretty.

"No, for real, dressed to impress," he reiterated.

"Shut up and drive," I joked to him as I got in his car. With every minute that passed on our way, I felt myself get more and more nervous.

"I'm not trying to sound like your dad here, Andie, but you know there's going to be alcohol at this party, right?" Ethan asked.

"I figured."

I knew my friends drank sometimes, but I'd never been around them when it was happening. I suddenly felt very grown up.

"So ... you're not gonna freak out if I have a beer? Or three?"

"No, Ethan." I knew he was alluding to my well-known typecast as a prude. "Maybe I'm done being such a goody-goody."

"Well stop the presses."

"No, honestly, I'm practically a senior now.

Maybe it's time I grow up."

"Geeze, you lie to your parents one time, and suddenly you're a rebel. Well, whatever you do, just please don't embarrass me in front of these guys."

"Ethan, come on, am I really that much of a killjoy?"

"Um ... sometimes, but I still love you."

I knew I was a rule-follower, but maybe I needed to lighten up a little bit. I was so preoccupied lately with ducking from Josh and plotting my survival for the next year, the thought of actually enjoying myself hadn't even entered my mind as an option. Maybe this party was my one chance to let it all go and celebrate my freedom, even if it did only last one night. And tomorrow I would rub off my makeup, don my creased baggy khakis, and see, or not see, Josh's car when I arrived at work as a reminder of just how *not* free I was from his silent chokehold. But that was tomorrow. And this was tonight.

When we pulled into the driveway, Ethan pointed to what looked like an old garage that stood about fifty feet from a small house, set against an array of pine trees.

"The loft is above the garage," he said, stepping out of the car. My stomach flipped. But not in the way I had been used to, no, this was different. Exciting. Ethan pushed open the door to the garage, and I followed him up a narrow, wooden staircase until we popped into the loft, which until then, I hadn't even been sure existed. It was, in a word, awesome. There were blinking Christmas lights strewn around the walls, a few dilapidated couches and armchairs set in a circle, heavy guitar amps and music equipment scattered about, and vintage band posters littered wherever there was empty wall space.

"You made it!" Carter shouted from across the room as we finished up the stairs, a red plastic cup in his hand. He slapped Ethan on the shoulder. "What's up brother," he said, seeming in a particularly good mood.

"Buzzed already? Damn dude. It's not even 8 PM!" Ethan laughed as he slapped Carter back on the shoulder. *Ah, of course, that's why Carter was so peppy.* I had to start learning these things.

"Andie!" Carter exclaimed, throwing his hands in the air as he came in for a hug. As he threw his arms around me in a jovial embrace, I could smell the alcohol over his natural scent of sandalwood and fresh linen, but on him, it smelled delicious. As he sloppily hugged me, his cheek grazed my face, and I felt the stubble from his jawline which made me shiver. Our bodies briefly touched, and I returned the hug, feeling his super soft zip-up hoodie against my skin. I had to remind myself to let go as he pulled back. "So glad you made it! Andie, have you met these guys?" he said, motioning toward a few people standing several feet behind him.

I recognized some of them from Intentionally Blank, but I'd never been introduced, so I shook my head. "This is Zach, Ryan, and Luca from the band, and this is Ryan's girlfriend, Krista." They all waved in my direction and continued chatting. "Get you guys a drink?"

"I'll take a beer," Ethan said. "Who else is coming tonight?" I could tell he was trying to change the subject to make me feel less awkward about having to say I didn't want a drink, but I shocked both Ethan and myself when I cut him off.

"I'll have whatever you're having, Carter," I said boldly.

"I like the way you think," he said as he stepped toward a table with several bottles and started mixing a drink.

"Dude, you sure?" Ethan whispered to me as Carter walked out of earshot. "I don't want to be responsible for what may or may not happen with Andie under the influence. I don't want your mom chasing me with a baseball bat or something."

"I'm all right," I shot back. I didn't know when, or if, I'd get another opportunity to feel this free over the next year. I was all in.

Carter came back and handed Ethan a can and me a cup. I took a sip and slyly spit it back out into the cup as soon as it hit my tongue. It tasted like gasoline and fire.

"Good? It's my favorite, a little mix of vodka, lime juice, and Sprite," Carter said.

"Great," I lied, taking another sip, forcing myself to swallow this time and trying painfully hard not to cringe. Ethan kicked me in the ankle. I knew he could tell my taste buds were miserable, but I ignored him.

"Anyway, nobody else is coming, man," Carter said, answering Ethan's earlier question. "It's just us."

"Where's Sloane?" I asked quickly, wishing I hadn't been so obviously bothered when I said her name.

"Far far away in Italy," Carter replied.

"Poor Carter, all alone," Ryan joked from behind us.

"Yeah now you know how we feel, like, all the time," Luca said, laughing.

Nobody else was coming. The only other girl there was someone else's girlfriend. I didn't have to exhaust myself competing for Carter's attention. I took another big sip of my drink, forgetting just how awful it was. I closed my eyes and went in for another swig.

"Slow down, Andie," Ethan whispered. "Pace yourself." But I didn't want to slow down. I wanted to throw myself into the moment, so I shut my eyes and downed the rest of my drink. I thrust my empty cup in front of Carter.

"Damn girl!" he said. "Care for another?"

I nodded, and he shuffled back to the table to start mixing me another disgusting cocktail.

"You sure you're okay?" Ethan asked me quietly.

"Please, Ethan, stop. I'm actually great. Better than I've been in a long time. Just let me have fun."

"Okay ... just checking."

Carter returned with a refill, and I could feel my mind starting to get a little fuzzy as my body began to feel warm. I suddenly had the urge to cut the bullshit and just talk to Carter like a real person. I pretended like he wasn't the star of every one of my daydream fantasies and I just plainly put my hand on his arm.

"So, Carter, what's your story?" I asked casually. I loved how cool I sounded, how calm I seemed. My nerves were melting away the flusher my cheeks got, and I took my jacket off as the room got hotter.

Ethan walked over to the others and joined in their conversation.

Carter motioned for me toward one of the worn-out couches, and we sat down next to each other, my legs crossed and him sitting deep back into the cushions.

"What's my story?" he repeated. "I guess my story is that I'm just a needy artist in a cool band with dreams of a big city, a killer record deal, and an epic love story," he said, his eyes sparkling. I was surprised at the honesty of his answer. "What about you? What's *your* story, Ms. Cavanaugh?" His words had started slurring a bit.

"Well," I said, taking a big sip of my awful drink. "I guess in that vein, I'm just a boring teenager with an excellent taste in music and a terrible taste in men." I laughed. I liked how fuzzy I was feeling, so I took another, bigger sip from my plastic cup.

"Well, your past taste in men may have been ... how do I say ... subpar? But you, Andrea Cavanaugh, are *anything* but boring." He tucked my hair behind my ear and every butterfly that ever existed in the natural world flooded into my stomach as my skin tingled and my heart fluttered.

We talked and drank for what felt like hours but was probably about forty-five minutes, swapping stories about our favorite live concert experiences, bonding over a shared agreement that Nicole was the absolute worst, and a surprisingly in-depth discussion about his parents' recent divorce. When Zach and Ethan came over and flopped onto the couch next to us, I had forgotten there were even other people at the party, and my surprise quickly changed to annoyance as I didn't want to stop talking to Carter.

"What're you guys up to over here?" Ethan asked, apparently getting tipsier by the minute.

"Oh, I'm just learning all about your friend Andrea," Carter said with a smile.

"Bo-ring!" Ethan yelled.

I wanted to smack him.

"You guys wanna play a drinking game? I got the cards," Zach asked, pulling out a deck of some type of cards I'd never seen before.

"Hell yes," Carter said, calling Ryan, Luca, and Krista over to the couches. Zach tried explaining the rules to me, but it was hard to understand as the fuzziness had taken over. But I tried my best, mostly copying whatever the person before me did, and drank when everybody shouted for me to drink.

By the end of the first game, I was laughing so hard I felt tears in my eyes. Ryan was dancing around ridiculously, and Krista was begging him to stop in between bursts of giggles.

"Round two! Deal 'em up!" Luca shouted. I wasn't sure how much more I could drink without giving in completely to the fuzziness. I pulled my hair into a loose ponytail as I felt sweat beading up on the back of my neck.

Halfway through the second round, Luca hopped up and turned up the music so loud we could barely even hear each other. The other guys abandoned the game and jumped up, joining Luca in a wild, semi-synchronized dance, almost falling over from laughter.

Krista leaned over to me and shouted over the music. "These idiots learned a dance to this song for Ryan's brother's wedding. They always freak out when it comes on. So embarrassing!" She giggled.

Ethan didn't know the dance but tried to keep up, which was the funniest part of all. When the song ended, they all dramatically fell to the floor. Someone turned the music down, and I headed over to the rickety table that was acting as the bar, trying to figure out how to make myself one of these horrible drinks.

Carter walked up next to me. "Meet me in the house, five minutes," he whispered, but before I could ask what or why, he made an announcement to the room.

"I'm heading inside to make a phone call. Be back soon. Don't stop the grooves though!" He started down the stairs, into the garage.

Nobody acknowledged him except Luca who yelled, "Tell Sloane we said hi!" He made mocking kissy noises.

Ethan was sprawled out on one of the couches, trying not to fall asleep as Zach talked to him.

I checked my phone. It had been one minute. I needed to wait four more. I didn't know what Carter wanted, but I didn't care, as long as it meant spending more time near him. When it had finally been five minutes, I headed toward the stairs, too, not announcing anything, assuming nobody would really notice. Luckily, I was right.

I got outside and walked quickly toward the sliding door of the house where I saw a light on. I slid the door open and slipped in, spotting Carter in the nearby kitchen. When he heard the door close, he came toward me and sat on the couch in the living room.

"So, this is your house?" I asked, trying to steady myself as I felt the room spin.

"Yeah, my dad works the night shift." I sat down next to him. "I love those guys, but I wanted a little more Andie time, hope that's okay," he said with that damn half smile that killed me every time.

"It's more than okay," I replied, surprised by my confidence. And even more surprised when I realized how *not* nervous I was.

"Can I ask you something?" he said.

"Of course." I liked that he wanted to know about me. I wasn't used to people asking *me* questions. It was usually the other way around.

"How could someone as beautiful as you date someone like that piano jerk?" He had a concerned look in his deep eyes. I didn't know what to say because I didn't know the answer myself. But I loved that he thought I was beautiful. I loved it more than I'd ever loved anything.

"I don't know. I just ... I think the romantic in me just thought I could make it work out." I looked down, feeling embarrassed when I remembered that Carter knew about the incident at the invitational.

"Well, that actually makes sense. I get it."

"You do?" I looked up. "I'm embarrassed. I just wish it never happened."

"Hey," he said, placing his smooth hand on the side of my face, his fingers in the back of my hair. I closed my eyes for a moment while I reveled in how good his touch felt. "Forgiven are the starry-eyed, for they know not why they love."

"That's beautiful." I returned his intense gaze. "Is that a song lyric?"

"No, well maybe, I'm working on something, but it's the truth. It's not your fault, Andrea. That guy sucks, okay? And what he did to you ... ugh. Seriously, when I look at you, you have such innocence in you, and that guy doesn't deserve you."

"Wow," I said in a breathy voice. I was living in one of my daydreams. And then Carter moved his face close to mine, closed his eyes, and kissed me, his soft lips meeting mine. I closed my eyes and melted into him. I put my hand on his rough stubbled face and kissed him back, as hard as I could. He ran his fingers through my hair and softly pulled my head back to kiss my neck, his tongue tracing my skin, which drove me wild. He was completely in control and knew exactly what to do. He pulled my body closer to his. Feeling pressed against his slender, strong body was mind-blowing and felt exactly as I'd always assumed it would feel, delicate yet powerful at the same time.

In a sudden decision, I placed one leg on one side of him, my knee on the couch, and pulled my other leg to the other side, straddling his lap as I kissed him with more passion than I ever even knew existed within me. I grinded my body into his as his hands clung to my back, pulling me even closer.

In one fell swoop, he stood up, still holding me and lifting me up with him. I stayed completely wrapped around him as he walked, still holding me, toward his bedroom at the end of the hall. We continued kissing as he walked, bumping into the doorway before finally laying me gently on his bed in the dark room. He slid down next to me, and we were both suddenly more sober than we'd ever been as he traced my face with his gentle finger.

"You are incredible, Andrea." His warm breath echoed off my skin as I absorbed every second, every feeling. I went to kiss him again, but he pulled back. "Just let me look at you," he said softly, his eyes settling on me as his hands wrapped around my body. I'd never felt so safe, so adored. I knew that this night would only lead to difficult questions with more difficult answers when the sun rose, but I tried not to let myself overthink this perfect moment.

He pulled my dress up and moved his hand underneath the fabric, caressing my bare skin, but it wasn't scary. It was breathtaking. I would've given myself completely to him if he'd asked.

He began kissing me again, sometimes softly and sometimes fiercely, pressing his body against mine, his hands all over me. It wasn't rough, it wasn't painful, it was ... magical. And every slight movement drove me more and more wild. I wasn't scared. I wasn't uncomfortable. I just wanted more and more.

"You drive me crazy," he said. I started laughing. "What's funny?" he asked.

I hadn't meant to laugh. It was just the only thing that came out when I started realizing how perfectly relaxed and unrestricted I felt. "I'm just ... I'm in awe, and I feel really good. Like, really good." I was disappointed in my lack of ability to articulate my feelings, but I hoped he knew what I meant.

He smiled and kissed me again. After a while, he pulled his head back and asked if he could just hold me. I agreed and turned around so he could spoon me, his arms wrapped around my waist and his head nestled behind mine. "I'm so into you," he whispered.

I closed my eyes and felt myself start to get emotional as I realized how much Josh had stolen from me, not just in our relationship but in the fear he held over me through his threats. This night with Carter, this is how I was supposed to be spending my life. Not constantly looking over my shoulder and terrified of someone who supposedly once cared about me. I swallowed the sadness and felt Carter hold me tightly, like he didn't want to let me go either.

We fell asleep like that, and a couple of hours later I woke up suddenly, sitting up.

"Whoa, what's wrong?" Carter asked, awoken by my quick movement.

"Nothing, I think..." I said, suddenly realizing I needed to tie up some loose ends. "I just need to tell my friend I'm not coming over tonight." I started looking for my phone.

"It's right here." He grabbed my cell from the floor, handing it to me and coaxing me to lay back down so he could put his arms around me again.

I happily obliged. As he wrapped himself around me, I opened the screen on my phone to text Stephanie and saw there were three texts from Josh. My heart sank. It was as if he knew I was happy somewhere.

"Ugh, what does *he* want?" Carter asked, peering at the phone over my shoulder.

"I don't know," I stammered, opening the messages.

Josh: Hi.

Twenty minutes later, after not hearing back, another text had come through.

Josh: Where R U?

Then there was a final message.

Josh: Hmm ... I see how it is.

"What does that mean?" Carter asked, sounding annoyed. "Is he still bothering you?"

"Sometimes." I sighed, not knowing how to

explain the hold he had on me. If I told Carter about the threats, would he realize how much baggage I had and decide it wasn't worth the trouble? Or would he try and do something about it and get caught in the crossfire? I couldn't risk either scenario. And I couldn't text Josh back now, in the middle of the night, because I knew he'd be upset if he thought I was out this late. I'd have to tell him I went to bed early and missed his messages.

I opened a text to Stephanie.

Me: Hey, may not make it to your place tonight but don't worry—all good. Thx for covering for me.

I then texted Ethan.

Me: Got caught up talking to Carter in the house—all good. Will meet you back in the loft in the morning. Maybe we can get breakfast before home?

Then I turned my phone off, tossing it back to the floor. I still had a few more hours until I had to re-enter reality.

"Carter, you are ... I don't even know what to say to you. You're gorgeous ... and fun ... and smart and I just ... I feel so lucky right now."

He smiled. "That's sweet. Thank you."

"When are we going to talk about ... you know..."

"Not yet," he said quietly. "When the sun rises, we'll figure everything out. Until then, just be here with me. Okay?"

"Okay," I agreed, feeling both so lost and so perfectly found. It was as if Carter knew a part of me that I didn't even know, and he introduced me to myself that night. And I was happy to find out that I was actually pretty great.

We talked a while longer, kissed a lot more, and told each other a list of things we found sexy about each other. I concentrated on his style, his jawline, and his hair. He chose my lips, my skin, and my eyes, which he said were haunting. When the sun cruelly started peeking into his bedroom window, he sighed and slowly sat up.

"All right," he said reluctantly. "I guess we should talk."

I sat up next to him, pulling the blanket over my lap and smoothing out my hair. "Yeah, I guess we should. So ... the elephant in the room, I'll just say it. What about Sloane?"

He sighed deeply. "Things haven't been good with Sloane for a long time. She's just ... she's not right for me. We've just been together forever, since we were practically kids. I should've ended it a long time ago, but I didn't want to hurt her, and I just let it go on way too long. And then she went abroad, and I felt like I could breathe again. I'm going to end it, I am. But I owe it to her to do it face-to-face, so when she gets back, I'll tell her, I promise. Well, I won't tell her about *this* necessarily, but I *will* break up with her. I need to. It's been a long time coming."

"Wow. Okay, well, if you're sure..."

"I'm sure. But I mean, I don't want to be a cheater, that isn't me. But you just ... I can't help myself when I'm around you. I'm crazy about you, Andie." I felt my heart swell as I smiled back at him. "Last night was everything. But I can't do this again until I break up with Sloane. I don't want to be that guy."

"I understand," I said genuinely, falling for him even more for being such a good human.

"But let's just, you know, keep in touch this summer. And when she gets back, I'll end things, and then I'll call you, and we'll see what happens..." He trailed off as he brought his face close to mine and kissed me softly on the lips.

"I feel like this isn't real..." I said, closing my eyes tightly.

"Open your eyes, beautiful," he said, his hand stroking my cheek. "This is very, very real."

Chapter Twenty-Two

By the time I got to work, I was drained but elated. I wore the dark circles under my eyes like a badge of honor. Carter and I had decided we'd tell the guys from the loft party that we got caught up talking in the house and passed out until morning. We didn't want word to get out about our night of passion until he was able to break up with Sloane. I finally had a secret that was fun to keep.

As I settled in at the clubhouse for my shift, I yawned and turned around to see Josh standing at the bar, apparently waiting for me.

"Whoa! How long have you been standing there?"

"A while." He did not look well. "Why didn't you text me back?"

Shit, I said to myself. My mind had been completely overtaken that morning by welcome, reminiscing flashbacks from the night before. I was consumed with visions of Carter carrying me to his bedroom. It was as if I could still feel his lips and hands on my body. I had completely forgotten about Josh's message. "I'm sorry, Josh, I fell asleep early and then was scrambling to get to work. It slipped my mind."

"How convenient," he said, his voice dripping with sarcasm. "I just miss you. Is it so much to ask to get a response? Are you ... avoiding me?" His voice rose.

"No, of course not." I knew I had to diffuse the situation quickly before it escalated. "I miss you too," I lied, hoping that a compliment would appease him.

"Just because we're not together doesn't mean I don't care about you. I wasn't trying to scare you. It's just important you know how much you mean to me."

"Thank you." I was disgusted at myself for thanking someone for hurting me, but knowing that it was the fastest way to end the conversation.

"You're still my good girl, right?" he asked in a baby voice, extending his hand open on top of the bar, expecting me to hold it. I did.

"Yes."

"Good." He squeezed my hand. I was nauseous. His hands felt clammy. Not like Carter's, which were smooth and gentle, yet strong. I wanted to be back in Carter's arms, under his blankets, feeling his breath.

A golfer came up to the bar and Josh dropped my hand.

"Sparkling water with lime, please," the golfer requested, eyeing Josh, who looked very out of place in a country club with his faded jeans and bright purple Grateful Dead t-shirt.

I nodded and began pouring the drink. "I'll talk to you soon, okay?" I said to Josh, hoping he would get the hint without being offended.

"You know it," he said with a wink that made my stomach turn. I had forced a smile before he walked off. After I had served the golfer his drink, I sat down and put my head in my hands. How could I make things happen with Carter if Josh was going to be constantly in the background? Josh would be furious if he found out about Carter. It felt like if Josh couldn't have me, nobody could have me.

"Who's gonna want you now?" His words from the car flashed back in my mind as they often did. But this time they stung a little less because I knew the answer. And it was a pretty great answer.

I knew I couldn't ignore my problem with Josh forever, but I pushed it out of my mind for the moment so I could relive the night before again. I closed my eyes and lost myself in the recent memory, flashes of tangled limbs and kind words. I let my body unclench, and the butterflies came back as I pictured Carter's face and remembered the way his hair felt between my fingers.

"Excuse me?" a customer interrupted my thought, and I quickly opened my eyes, jumping up to take his order, but keeping Carter tucked safely in the back of my mind while I worked.

When my shift ended, I practically floated to my car, high on the scent of sandalwood and fresh linen. As I drove home, I realized that I hadn't even noticed if Josh's car was in his driveway when I left, and I was proud of that.

When I got home, I saw a text message come through.

Carter: Thinking of you...

I sighed and pressed my phone against my chest, breathing in the feeling, adoring the butterflies as they so kindly fluttered deep under my skin. "Somebody," I whispered to myself as I now knew the answer to Josh's hurtful question. Somebody *did* want me. Maybe I wasn't as ruined as he wanted me to believe.

Chapter Twenty-Three

As the weeks of summer ticked by, things were starting to look up. I had only heard from Josh a couple of times, just short messages with easy answers, and I'd been texting back-and-forth with Carter almost every day. I loved reading his messages. He had such a poetic way with words, and knowing they were directed to me was still hard to comprehend, but I emphatically enjoyed every moment of trying.

When I woke up one Thursday morning, the day started like any other. My parents were at work, so I relaxed at home until my shift started at the clubhouse in the afternoon. I was sprawled out on the blue living room couch, texting with Carter about his upcoming Intentionally Blank show in Detroit. It was the biggest venue they'd ever played, so he was pretty excited, and I loved encouraging him.

When I heard the doorbell ring, I didn't think much of it. I never answered the door when I was home alone, so I ignored it and continued texting. But then the knocking started.

Me: Ugh someone at the door ... they won't leave.
Carter: That's annoying. You okay?
Me: Ya, they'll go away.
But they didn't go away.
"*Andrea*!"
I heard Josh's voice scream from outside. My heart dropped. It was as if he could sense when things were going well and knew just when to angrily scratch out any progress I had made.
"I see your car. I know you're there!"
I knew I had to open the door. Maybe I could calm Josh down, stroke his ego, and things would be

okay. I went toward the front door and opened it a crack.

When he felt the door start to move, he pushed it open with such force that I stumbled back.

"Whoa, it's okay, Josh. Hey why don't you sit down?" I tried to remain cheery and patient as if that could counteract his energy, while I closed the door behind him.

He flopped down on the couch. "Jesus took you long enough," he said.

"Sorry, I didn't know it was you. What's up?"

"Something has to be up for me to visit you?"

"No, of course not."

My phone chimed from the couch, and he peered down.

"Carter?" he said, looking at the missed text. "As in ... Carter Wells?"

"Yeah, we're friends, just through Ethan." I wondered if he could tell I was downplaying it.

"I don't know how I feel about that, Andie." Josh's eyes were bloodshot, and his hair was greasy. He looked like he'd been awake for days. I didn't say anything. "I don't know if I like my girl talking to all these guys. How's that supposed to make me feel?"

"Your girl? I thought..." I started but didn't know how to finish. We had broken up. I hadn't imagined that, had I? No, no, that memory was seared into my brain. I knew I wasn't mistaken, and I was frustrated that he could make me question such a thing.

"You thought what, baby?" he said, as if that were a perfectly reasonable thing to say after he'd threatened to kill me, told everyone he broke up with me, and then ghosted me for weeks.

"I thought ... you wanted ... I thought that you broke up with me," I stammered, remembering that that's how he'd wanted to spin it.

"So?" He sat up and stretched his arms out wide on the top of the couch cushions, looking relaxed. I was still standing on the other side of the room, tapping my fingers together in an attempt to distract my mind from the increasing tension.

My phone chimed again.

"Jesus this guy's really blowing you up, huh?" Josh picked up my phone.

I walked toward him with my hand outstretched to try and grab my phone, but he pulled it out of my reach and dangled it from his fingertips before he slid the screen open with his thumb. "Andie, everything ok?" he read aloud. "So Carter calls you Andie?" His voice sounding increasingly unstable as if I had somehow betrayed him.

"Everybody calls me that, it's just a nickname." My mind started racing as I felt the familiar alarms start ringing throughout my body.

Josh started scrolling through our conversation history. I made another quick reach for my phone, and he grabbed my forearm, gripping it hard as he read aloud again. "'Can't stop thinking about your smile.' Well, it sounds like you two are *very* good friends."

"Josh, please." I could feel in my gut that this was headed in a dangerous direction.

"Oh, fuck this guy. What is he, some wannabe poet or some shit like that? 'Your eyes haunt me, there's innocence in them, and your lips just beg to be kissed.'" Josh read in a sarcastic, mocking tone.

I felt like he'd taken these words from Carter that I'd read over and over again, that I'd memorized and adored, that I'd kept secret and filled my whole heart with, and defiled them with thick, black paint and angry brushstrokes. Carter's beautiful words that gave me light and hope, now vandalized with Josh's sharp, hate-filled tongue. I couldn't let him take this from me.

Josh tossed my phone to the other side of the couch and looked at me with wild eyes. "I thought you loved *me*," he said.

I didn't know how to play this. I opened my mouth, but nothing came out. I didn't love him. I had actually grown to hate him. His touch made me cringe. And his musty scent made my skin crawl.

"Did you think I was bluffing when I said I would kill you?" His voice had gone from sad and desperate to furious and scathing in a matter of seconds, and my lip quivered as my body shut down and entered the raw survival mode I'd sadly become familiar with.

My mind stopped racing, and an autopilot took over to just get me through this situation, even if it was second-by-second. This was the same autopilot that was present when I sat curled up by the lockers while books hurled at my head, or when the back of Josh's hand met my soft face with a painful force. It was even there when he forced his hands into me while I lay rigid and motionless next to him on his abrasive, unwashed sheets. I welcomed this autopilot, though, because it let me step outside of my fear momentarily. And then the emotions and feelings I would assign to the scene could come out later when it was safe and I was alone.

"I do love you," I heard myself say.

"Prove it," he sneered as he started unbuckling his belt. "You haven't slept with Carter, have you? Wait, don't answer, of course you haven't. Look who I'm talking to," he said, knowing my feelings about saving my virginity.

I closed my eyes and shook my head. I knew where this was going and I just wanted it to be over. I couldn't feel the anger and sadness that was building up in my heart, pumping itself into the rest of body like poison. I was numb.

My phone chimed from across the room, and I felt tears well behind my closed eyelids as I thought of Carter, trying to reach me, and having no idea I was sitting on this blue couch, preparing my body to betray him, to betray myself, as Josh grabbed the back of my hair. His other hand pulled my skirt up over my waist and stretched my panties to the side, so hard that the elastic band broke as he shoved himself into me.

I screamed. I'd never felt pain like that before. It was as if I was being ripped apart.

"You love it," Josh said, breathing heavily between thrusts, pulling my hair back harder with each motion. He started kissing my neck sloppily.

I could feel his saliva dripping off my skin, and I bit my lip hard to try and distract myself from the pain. It didn't occur to me to yell or to hit him or to beg him to stop. I knew better. If I did anything, things would get a lot worse, though at this point it was hard to imagine that that was possible.

I started counting in my head, and when that usual tactic didn't take my mind away from what was happening, I tried to think of song lyrics. I sang in my head, "Swim" by Jack's Mannequin, doing whatever I could to distract myself.

By the time I got to the second chorus, it was over.

Josh slumped on top of me, his clammy, sweaty skin felt cold against mine. When he finally peeled himself off of me, he stood up and began buckling his pants.

"Goddamn, you felt amazing," he said, as I pulled my skirt down and tried to sit up, even though every inch of my groin was burning and sore. "I hope Carter Wells enjoys my sloppy seconds." He let out a volatile laugh.

"I'll see you around, babe." And just like that, he was gone.

It wasn't until I heard his car drive off that I burst into tears. Explosive, uncontrollable tears. I felt disgusting, untouchable, and the musky scent that lingered on my skin was sickening. I ran to the bathroom and gagged, heaved into the toilet, but nothing came out. I turned the faucet on in the shower and sat curled up on the cold tile while the hot water ran, the steam fogging up the mirror and making me choke on my tears until I cut the heat with a stream of cool water.

I pulled myself into the shower and scrubbed my body as hard as I could, wanting every droplet of sweat and every essence of his body completely washed down the drain, into the gutter where it belonged. I hated myself as I scrubbed. I hated my body for tempting Josh from the beginning. I hated my mind for letting this happen, and most of all I just hated every part of me that Carter would never want to touch. I was used, violated, and nobody wanted a second-hand girlfriend.

When I finally got out of the shower, I dried myself off, wiped my eyes, and started getting ready for work. None of my clothes felt right, like my body didn't deserve to wear anything nice. I settled on the wrinkled, baggy pants I found in the back of my closet and threw on black, plastic flip flops with my work polo. I pulled my wet hair back into a tight bun and walked back into the living room, stopping when I saw the imprint in the plush, blue sectional. I swallowed hard and walked over, smoothing out the couch as if nothing had happened and as if nobody had been there.

I picked my phone up and saw five missed texts from Carter.

Carter: Who was at the door?
Carter: Are you okay?

Carter: Starting to get a little worried...

Carter: If I don't hear from you in five minutes, I'm coming over.

Carter: I'm on my way.

I wasn't prepared to account for what had just happened yet. I hadn't decided what I would tell Carter if anything. And before I could think, I heard a knock on the door.

"Andrea, it's Carter, are you there?"

I heard his worried voice from outside. The guilt was piercing. He was so kind and lovely, and I was so vile and unworthy of his attention. I wondered how, or when, he would come to learn that, too.

I opened the door. "I'm so sorry. My phone died in the middle of our conversation, and I plugged it in, and I guess I forgot..." I was stumbling, without a clue of where I was going.

"But you ... took a shower?" he said, confused, pointing to my wet hair as he walked into the house.

God, he smelled good.

"Um, yeah, I have to go to work in an hour."

"Who was at the door? I was really worried, Andie." He gently put his hands on my shoulders.

"Uh, nobody, just someone selling something." I couldn't look at him in the eyes.

"Who? Selling what?" he pressed, sensing my deceit. "Have you been crying?" He tried to focus on my swollen eyes. He touched my chin and lifted my head, so I met his gaze. "Hey, Andie, talk to me."

But I couldn't. He didn't deserve to get pulled into the mess I had created. Carter's only fault was falling for such a broken girl.

Forgiven are the starry-eyed, for they know not why they love, I thought to myself before answering him with another lie. Carter would be forgiven for having feelings for me. He could move on to anyone else in the line of girls dying to be close to him. And in a few days or even moments, I'd be forgotten as he softly touched the face of someone else and wrote graceful songs about other girls' equally haunting eyes. But I couldn't be forgiven for what I had done. The innocence he loved in my eyes was gone, removed with force. And I'd never be the same.

Chapter Twenty-Four

When I got to work that day, Josh's car was not in his driveway. It provided little comfort because he was already everywhere. His scent was burned into my skin like a scarlet letter. I tried to push aside the feelings of guilt I carried for leaving Carter with little answers. I pictured him driving home from my house, confused and frustrated, which made me ache. I swallowed hard, trying to push down the discomfort, but it took a few tries before I could focus on my surroundings and start serving drinks to waiting golfers.

When the crowd of customers died down, and I found myself in a quiet lull, I felt the panic creeping into my chest. I wasn't ready to face the emotions yet and hoped I could hold them off a little bit longer, but as the sorrow and anxiety began bubbling through my veins, I knew this time it was too big for me to carry alone. I needed help. But I didn't know who could help me. I would never tell my parents. The thought of them looking at me through a different lens, a tainted and foggy lens where they could barely recognize the girl they raised with high morals and good manners, I couldn't bear that. I wanted to tell Stephanie, but I was afraid she'd make a scene with the anger she'd feel toward Josh, and I didn't want to draw more attention to something I had hoped to shroud in silence until my last breath. So nervously I texted Harper.

Me: Can you come over after work?

Harper: Not tonight. Sorry, chica—tomorrow morning?

Me: Okay.

Harper: Everything all right?

Me: Ya, just want to hang out.

I lied, not wanting to get into it over text. This was better. It'd give me more time to decide what I needed to say to remove the burden of isolation, to hopefully get just enough of this oppressive weight off my chest so I could breathe, even if only shallowly. Plus, if Harper came tomorrow morning, my parents would be at work so we'd have more freedom to be candid. I could cry, and maybe she would hug me. That sounded really nice.

And then logic hit me, suddenly, and forcefully—I had just had unprotected sex. And there was a lot that came with that, pregnancy being my first concern. And I refused to let this situation define me any more than it already had. I wasn't eighteen yet, so I couldn't buy the morning after pill at the drugstore, but I knew of a small women's clinic downtown that I'd been to with Stephanie before to pick up her birth control. I figured they would be able to help me, or at least know what to do.

I tried to keep myself distracted throughout the rest of my shift and practically sprinted to my car when Rebecca showed up to relieve me. I needed to get this over with.

When I pulled into the parking lot at the clinic, I sat in my car for a few minutes, bracing myself to talk to a stranger about what had happened to me. I couldn't bring myself to say the "r-word." Not only had I not said no or tried to fight Josh off, but if I ever uttered the word "rape" in public and it somehow got reported to the police, I would be humiliated and scorned. Not to mention, I'd also be ridiculed for even thinking such a thing had happened when the story, on paper, shows me practically being a willing participant. And I had no proof otherwise. It'd be my word against Josh's, and the one truth I knew, the one constant that repeatedly pounded through my veins, was that Josh would always win. Disgusted with myself, I made the long walk from my car to the front desk of the clinic, tapping my fingers together and trying to think of how to most articulately explain what I needed without assigning any emotion to my words, so as not to raise alarm.

"Can I help you?" the receptionist asked.

I stared at her, frozen. The burden of that question stuck in my mind, causing me to pause. A sudden urge took over me to just unload all of it, confess my transgressions of silence and Josh's violent outbursts. But I swallowed to push it down and began speaking the words I had practiced in the car.

"Nothing was supposed to happen," I said. That part felt important. I tasted the other words, the confessions, as they itched on the back of my tongue, but I cleared my throat, swallowed harder, and continued. "But ... I need the morning after pill." I exhaled my relief for having gotten through the sentence.

"Are you eighteen?" she asked plainly.

"No."

"Fill out this form and wait in there." She gestured to a small waiting room nearby that was littered with outdated magazines and poorly cushioned folding chairs. I followed her orders and sat down, staring at the form. I began writing in the standard answers—name, date of birth, phone number, and then it got complicated.

"How many sexual partners have you had?" The question mocked me from the page. I didn't have an acceptable answer. Did it mean like actual sex? If so, I guess one. But I didn't want to count that one. If it included making out and fooling around, then that'd be two, and I really wanted to count that one.

"Have you ever been sexually abused or forced to have sex against your will?" I felt anger rise in my body because I didn't know how to answer this one, either. I wanted just to write "it's complicated," but settled with scribbling a question mark and moving on. I felt like everybody in the waiting room was staring at me, so I took a quick inventory of their faces to ensure nobody was familiar.

Before I could get farther in my form, a nurse called my name, and I was grateful to get away from the judging strangers. She escorted me into a cold, sterile room with pamphlets on the wall displaying diverse, smiling people next to scary words, and she motioned for me to sit down as she opened a new chart on the bare countertop.

"Date of birth?" she asked, her voice sounding annoyed already. She was a heavyset woman with thick gray roots peeking out from under her otherwise mousey brown hair. She had deep frown lines carved into her face and thick eyebrows that seemed always to be furrowed with frustration. She never made eye contact.

I told her my birthdate and sat tense, waiting for the next question.

"Here for the morning after pill?" I nodded. "Did you use protection?" she asked, still nose deep in the chart.

"No," I said quietly. She let out a long sigh and shook her head, walking to a white cabinet on the wall.

"Kids today," she grumbled to herself. "You *always* use protection. Understand?" Her tone was belittling as she pulled a handful of assorted colored condoms out of the cabinet and shoved them in a brown paper bag, thrusting the bag in my direction.

"Nothing was supposed to happen," I said meekly, as I'd practiced, hoping she'd recognize something genuine in my voice and give me the empathy I so desperately craved.

But she scoffed instead. "Yeah, like I haven't

heard that one before." She laughed sarcastically under her breath.

I wanted to dig a hole in the tile floor of that clinic, climb inside, and bury myself deep into the earth where nobody could find me. There was officially nobody left to trust. "I don't need these," I said, trying to hand the paper bag of condoms back to her. Accepting that bag made me feel like I was expecting this to happen again, and this was never going to happen again.

"Yeah, heard that one before, too," she said rolling her eyes and waving off my gesture with a tired hand. "You're all set." She scribbled some notes in the chart. "Pick your pill up at the front. And next time, use protection," she snapped as she exited the room.

I sat in silence for a moment, clutching the paper bag awkwardly in my hands, feeling the material crinkle in my grip. I made my way to the front desk where the receptionist gave me a purple box containing the morning after pill. She told me that since I was underage, I could pay on a donation basis, so I pulled a $10 bill out of my wallet and slid it under the bulletproof glass that she sat behind before I turned around to leave.

As I pushed the exit door open, the fresh air hit my face and I diverted my eyes from the sun. I started what felt like a long walk back to the parking lot, shuffling quickly in hopes nobody nearby would see me.

Before I'd made it ten steps, I heard the clinic door squeak open and footsteps jogging behind me. My shoulders tensed and pulled away when I felt a hand on my shoulder. Turning around meekly, I was surprised to see the receptionist in her bright blue scrubs.

"Sorry, I just thought you might want this?" She held out a small lavender business card and placed it in my hand before I could say anything. "Look, I'm not a doctor or a nurse or anything and not really supposed to be offering advice, but this is a card for a therapist. A really good one. She saved my life after I was raped. "

"I wasn't..." I started.

"I know," she cut me off. "It's okay. Just ... just don't throw it away, okay?"

I nodded, pursing my lips, trying not to cry. How did she know? Was I that pathetic that it was written all over my face? I shoved the card into my back pocket, hoping it would disappear.

"I have to get back inside. This place isn't the best for this kind of stuff. If you need medicine or whatever, then sure, but if you need something else ... just call her okay?" She turned and jogged back inside, heading back to her post behind the thick bulletproof glass.

I watched through the glass door as she sat down at her computer, shuffling through some forms on the desk as if nothing had happened. The card in my pocket felt like it was burning my skin, so I closed my eyes, trying to ignore the discomfort. I couldn't comprehend what she had just said or why she had said it, so I swallowed and refocused on getting back to my car and getting out of here as quickly as I could.

When I got into my car, I surprised myself with how collected I was. My eyes burned with the urge to cry, but I flipped my hair over my shoulder, took a deep breath, and started driving. The paper bag of condoms screamed at me from the passenger seat. I couldn't take it home. Not just because I didn't want my parents to see it, but because I didn't want it anywhere near me.

"This will never happen again," I said to myself, out loud this time. I didn't know how I would accomplish that yet, but I couldn't do it again. I was already reminded every time I went to the bathroom when specs of blood appeared on the toilet paper as I wiped where my skin had been torn. I was reminded every time I winced upon sitting, feeling like someone had hit a baseball bat between my legs. And I couldn't take another reminder, which is what this bag would be, even if it sat in the back of my bedside drawer. I would know it was there, waiting to be used, like a cruel stopwatch counting down to my next nightmare.

When I got into my neighborhood, I drove past my house and up a hill on the next street over, parking on a curb near an opening in a small forest of pine trees. I used to come here all the time when I was younger, exploring the clearing with other neighborhood kids, pretending to be uncovering ancient ruins and dinosaur bones as we'd prod the dirt and grass with long sticks. I hadn't been here in years, but it felt somehow appropriate, safe. The summer day was cooling down as the sunlight started to dim, so I grabbed the paper bag and got out of the car, carrying it through the clearing and remembering to turn left and walk a short way until I came across a tiny manmade pond. I remembered it being so much bigger when I was little, but now it just looked like a sad, swampy puddle. Brushing some stray dirt off an old, sunken log, I sat down and opened the bag, letting the brightly colored condoms sealed tight in plastic wrappers spill out onto the dirt and grass. I counted them. There were nine condoms. I picked up a purple one and looked at it carefully. It felt like I was holding something powerful in my hand, as if this stupid purple condom represented one vile, forceful session that I was somehow preventing by destroying this physical manifestation of intent. I threw the condom as far as I could, aiming at the sad, swampy pond, and I smiled when it landed amidst the algae and lily pads. Small, buzzing black flies flew close to the surface, and the plastic purple wrapper looked suddenly much more fitting amidst the dirty water. I picked up the green one next, and before I could feel the slippery texture, I threw it, too, toward the pond, harder this time. I stood up to get a better aim and grabbed the next one, yellow, hurling it as far away from my body as I could get it. I walked closer to the edge of the water and let the remaining condoms fall straight down from my hand. I watched them float gently atop the dark water, flecks of dirt staining their rainbow wrappers as they glided away from me, some getting tangled in the thick weeds growing from the muck below and some continuing to drift atop the water, heading toward the muddy shoreline.

When I ran out of condoms, I crumpled the paper bag into a small wad and let it drop at my feet, stepping on it with my right foot and twisting it underneath my shoe, letting it rip and disappear under the thick, dark dirt.

Satisfied, I sighed and sat back down on the log, looking out over the pond, content with my decisions as I watched the colored wrappers fade into the murky water. I stayed there for a few minutes, breathing in the pine-scented air.

I told myself I had very few options now. I could just exist and accept that this was my life from now on. I'd be broken, but at least I'd be alive. Or I could purposely enrage Josh to the point where he did kill us both as he'd so articulately promised, that way I wouldn't have to live with the disgust that clung to my skin and invaded my sense of being, and he couldn't hurt anyone else ever again. In either scenario, I would sacrifice any future I had with Carter, whether that be one more fleeting night or an eternity of romantic gestures and perfect hair. I would never know what it could've been. But on the other hand, he would never have to know how truly impure and damaged I now was. And he could think of me fondly, my memory preserved as the girl with haunting, innocent eyes with whom he shared a few blissful, passion-filled moments. Maybe he'd be sad briefly, but I hoped he'd know deep down that I did this to protect him and give him the future he wanted with a girl who actually deserved him. Not a mess with red highlights who, while he texted her sweet messages from his bedroom across town, let her sweaty ex-boyfriend defile her on a lumpy blue couch late one summer morning.

When I stood up to head back to my car, I remembered the business card in my pocket. I took it out and studied it, my finger tracing over every word.

"Stacey Hawthorne, LCSW." This was followed by, "Individual, Group and Family Therapy." There was a phone number and address. The font was pretty, and the card was thick. I started to crumple it in my hand but hesitated and smoothed it back out, rereading the words. I couldn't throw it away and watch the delicate lavender card float amongst the disgusting condoms in the dirty pond. I decided to save it, at least for a little while. It would be easy enough to hide. Even if I never called Stacey Hawthorne, LCSW, I could look back at this card and remember that someone once saw me, and someone once reached out. And with that small gesture and this creased business card, there was hope.

Chapter Twenty-Five

The next day I was still sore. I was nervous for Harper to come over, but I decided I would tell her what happened. She was my best friend, and I thought, hoped, that she could help protect and advise me. She liked Josh so I knew she wouldn't cause a scene like Stephanie might. She would keep my secret.

After my parents had headed to work, I began to get ready, and my phone chimed. I cringed, praying it wasn't Josh and sighed with relief when I saw Carter's name instead.

Carter: How are you? Kinda worried about you. Should I be?

I wanted to tell him there was a lot to be concerned about: my sanity, my general well-being, and the future of our might-be-could-be one-day relationship. I didn't text any of that though.

Me: All good, don't worry. Xoxo.

I wanted to fiercely protect Carter from becoming collateral damage in the war I had caused. He deserved to be shielded from the bloodshed and continue living in a space where men were kind and gentle, and women dreamt of love instead of plotting plans of escape.

When Harper came to the door, I tried to stay calm as I walked her up to my bedroom. She flopped on the end of the bed and started chatting about the new roommate she'd been assigned to in her dorm and how their first phone call was.

I wasn't listening. Instead, I grabbed my purse from my bedside table and dumped the contents onto the bed in front of her lap. A silver wallet, burgundy lip gloss, some loose change, scented hand sanitizer, and a long cardboard box labeled "Plan B" fell amidst the comforter.

Harper stopped mid-sentence and jumped off the bed, standing and pointing at the purple box. "What the hell is this?" she said before turning her confused gaze to me. "What did you do, Andrea?"

"I need your help."

"Holy shit."

"Please don't get mad. I need you right now," I begged. Harper didn't say anything, just stared at me, waiting for me to continue. "Nothing was supposed to happen." Those words had become familiar as they rolled off my tongue.

"Okay, but what *did* happen?" Her voice was growing impatient, which made me unsure if this was the right decision after all, but I pressed on.

"Josh came over yesterday."

"No ... no way."

"He was upset, and ... nothing was supposed to happen. But it did. And I don't know what to do. I got this pill, but I don't even know how to take it. And I'm scared," I said quickly, my sentences all running together. But it was out, and I briefly felt relieved, like I had shone a light onto the sliver of the darkness that weighed down my body. But my relief was quickly halted as Harper's reaction turned from surprise to anger.

"He was upset ... so you *fucked* him?"

"No. It wasn't like that."

"Well, you don't get a morning after pill for having a polite conversation, Andie. So..."

"Never mind," I said, completely regretting my decision as my face turned warm. I had always told myself nobody would understand, and I should've listened to that instinct. I had hoped Harper would be an exception, but she was just like everybody else. There would be no saviors here. I would not be absolved. And I would have to let that sink in, as raw and unnatural as it felt.

Harper grabbed the purple box and tore it open, popping two pills out of their plastic casing and putting them in my hand. "Take these now."

"Are you sure? Just like that?"

"Yes, I'm sure, just do it," she said aggressively.

I placed the pills on my tongue and swallowed, feeling them push slowly down my dry throat as I swallowed again, trying to force them down faster.

"I gotta go," Harper said, her eyes watering as she rushed toward the doorway.

"Harper, please." I desperately wanted for her to understand what happened. How I didn't want him on top of me. How I sang the lyrics to "Swim" in my head when the counting wasn't enough. How Carter helplessly texted me while I was pinned down, trying not to cry out in pain. But she just left. When I heard the front door close behind her, I sat on my bed, more alone than I'd ever, ever been.

I laid down on top of my blankets, curling my knees to my chest, defeated. I had hours until I had to be at work, and I was terrified of my thoughts. Not wanting to be alone with wherever my mind was darkly drifting to, I closed my eyes and tried to replace the invading thoughts with whatever I could think of to distract myself until I fell asleep.

I awoke with a gasp to a loud, banging knock at the front door, my heart leaping into my throat as I tried to get my bearings. I checked the clock. I'd been asleep for over an hour.

"Andrea, open the door!" Josh shouted from outside.

I ran down the stairs and pulled the curtain in the foyer aside to see him standing there. "I won't," I said through the door, suddenly feeling brave since things couldn't get a lot worse.

"Andie, please open the door." His voice had softened. "I'm not mad, and I won't touch you, I just need to talk." Something was comforting about that statement. It was as if he admitted that him touching me was a bad thing, like he knew I didn't want him to. And there was a cheap vindication in that.

I cracked the door open. "Talk."

"Please let me come in. It's important."

I sensed an urgency in his voice. Maybe he was coming to apologize, to beg for my forgiveness?

As I pondered whether I should take the risk or not, he slipped his hand through the crack and pressed the door open, walking in quickly, taking fast, heavy, exaggerated steps. I closed the door behind him and pressed my back up against it, my left hand steady on the doorknob.

"Why did you have to tell her?" he asked, his eyes wet and distressed.

"Tell who?"

"Harper. Why did you tell Harper about yesterday? That was a private moment between you and me. That was *private*, Andrea. I was thinking all day about how incredible you felt, and then Harper comes over, screaming at me." He walked closer to me, so close I could feel his breath, and put his hand on my waist.

My body tensed and I closed my eyes.

"I mean, how am I supposed to say no to you?" He tightened his grip on my waist. His words were sickening, and I felt my stomach churn as he spoke. "You're so goddamn sexy, and after yesterday, I can't get you out of my head. But you had to open your mouth, and now you've fucked this all up."

"I don't understand." I opened my eyes just

barely.

He let go of me and turned around, running his hands through his messy brown hair. "Harper and I ... are together." He was unable to look me in the eyes as he spoke.

"What do you mean?" I knew exactly what he meant, but I needed him to say it out loud.

"We are together. We have been for a long time. The first time Harper and I had sex, you and I had been dating only a couple of months, and it just, I don't know, it just kinda blew up. I think I love her. And I know that's shitty because this all happened when you and I were together, but I promised her it was over with you. And now she's beyond pissed at me for fucking you." He spoke fast. His words sliced into me, one by one, as I comprehended what they each meant.

"Wh-when I was your girlfriend ... you were ... sleeping with ... my best friend?" I was barely able to get the words out, my nausea escalating to where I could taste the bile in the back of my throat.

"Yes, but it wasn't just like that. I mean, not *just* physical. We have a real connection, Andie. Nobody gets me like Harper."

I couldn't believe what I was hearing. Was Josh looking for sympathy? I tasted the hot, salt from my tears as they streamed out of my eyes. I walked into the living room to sit down, realizing I was now sitting on the edge of the blue couch that's recent history felt as though it now defined me.

He followed and sat next to me, wrapping his arm around my shoulders as if he was trying to comfort me.

I didn't have the energy to push it off.

He continued. "Look, I said I know this is shitty, okay? This has been tearing me up all year." I was waiting for him to apologize, to realize what this was doing to me, but in true Josh fashion, he focused solely on himself as he spoke. "I just ... I don't want to ruin things with her. She's incredible, but look, we both know Harper, so let's be honest. She's not very fuckable, right?"

I stared at him with a cold, somber glare. I had no words to express the tidal wave of anger and sadness that was brewing inside of me.

"But you, Andie ... we may not have a lot in common, but I can't get enough of your body." I stood up, not wanting his arm around me anymore. I thought I was going to be sick, but I swallowed the hot, acidic saliva that kept forcing its way up. "Yesterday was supposed to be just between us, and now you may have ruined everything."

"Fuck. You." I whispered, shocked by my own words, but suddenly inspired by how good they felt coming out.

"Ex*cuse* me?" He stood up slowly to meet my gaze.

"Nothing." I looked down as I felt my newfound bravery retreat.

"That's what I thought."

Chapter Twenty-Six

Josh left my house shortly after his confession. I wasn't sure what he was hoping to gain by telling me, but perhaps he felt relieved of the secrecy now, having dumped it on me like an anchor. I couldn't go to work that day. I had to figure things out, get my head on straight, calm my body down. I called Rebecca and asked if she could cover for me. Worried that she'd be angry for taking a double shift, I was pleasantly surprised when she happily agreed, bragging about how much she'd increase her tips.

I had barely hung up with Rebecca when I dialed Harper.

"Hello?" she said casually.

"I know everything." I felt my chin quiver.

"What are you talking about?" Her tone rose to an uncomfortably chipper level.

"Cut the shit, Harper. I *know*."

"Andrea, I don't know what you're talking about. Know what?"

"I know you slept with my boyfriend!" I screamed into the phone, hating how much I sounded like a cheap cliché.

She paused. "I'll be over in a minute," she said quietly, with defeat.

I hung up and waited for her, my blood boiling more with every passing minute. I didn't know what I would say to her when she arrived. There was no resolve I was hoping for. And I didn't want Josh to get the satisfaction of us fighting over him after he pitted us against each other in the first place.

When the doorbell rang, I felt something I didn't expect. I felt sorry for Harper. And as I walked to the door, my strategy changed. When I turned the handle, she burst through, her face beet red and her voice shaking.

"I'm so sorry, Andie. I'm so sorry," she kept repeating.

And then I hugged her.

She pushed me away. "I'm a monster. I'm so sorry."

I hugged her again, and this time she let me but didn't return the embrace. We stood there awkwardly for a few moments, my arms wrapped around her while she stood straight and tense, sobbing.

"Shh, Harper, just come sit down," I said, waving her into the living room. This time I sat on a nearby armchair. I couldn't feel the fabric on that blue couch again today.

She sat on the edge of the couch, burying her face in her hands.

"Look, Harper ... I don't know what to say, but this doesn't need to be a big fight."

She wiped her nose with her sleeve and looked up at me, her eyes pink and swollen. "Wh-what do you mean?"

"I mean, this ... you and me ... our friendship, I think this is over. I think we're done here. And maybe we have been for a while. But look, you win. Josh is yours. But he's already cheated on us both, Harper, and you may not know this yet, but he is a bad, bad guy." She looked down and didn't speak. "So that's it." I stood up, waiting for her to do the same.

She slowly rose to her feet and began walking toward the door. "You're my best friend," she said quietly, the words causing her to break into tears again.

"Right. Bye, Harper." I pointed to the door.

"No, Andie, I'm sorry, I'll do anything."

"I think we both know that's not true," I said with a small sigh.

She continued sobbing as she left. I wondered what she thought about as she got into her car. Did she regret her decision to choose Josh over me? Was she happy to have this out in the open? Was she angry that Josh was still attracted to me? But none of it mattered. I was finished with Harper Cooley, and I was a little disappointed in myself for how easy of a decision it was. But maybe deep down I had always known. And this, their affair, was something I was only a witness to, not the cause. I didn't feel guilty. I didn't feel ashamed. I was just hurt. But then I realized ... this could be my way out. While I had gotten rid of Harper in a single conversation, it had not been so easy to break free of Josh's steel grip. But I had an idea.

I picked up my phone and dialed Stephanie.

"Well hello, love," she answered.

"Steph, something has happened."

"*What?*" she said, sensing the despair in my voice. And I poured out every detail of Josh and Harper's affair and ongoing relationship that I could remember. I purposely left out the details I could not yet face myself—the sex, the threats, the abuse, I didn't share those stories. That was something I would have to live with, and one day die with, too. It would be my guilt, my indignity, to wear forever. But this, Josh and Harper's secret forbidden relationship, this was something I could shine a light on to anyone who was willing to look. It could, perhaps, result in some solid proof against their heinous behavior, even though it wouldn't cover everything.

"Oh no, hell no." Her voice got angrier with each syllable. "How dare they? I mean ... how *dare* they? Who do they think they are? They will *not* get away with this,

Andrea."

Stephanie only used my full name when she was serious. This was it. She could be the key to getting Josh out of my life. I teared up as I began to imagine a Josh-free life. I pictured going out without looking over my shoulder, eating a meal without feeling sick, and getting dressed without worrying about looking too good or not good enough. I could even spend time with who I wanted when I wanted, and not have to think about the way my goddamn fork sounded against my teeth. It didn't seem possible to get all of that back, especially since I had just started to accept that this was my life now, this inescapable, vicious cycle.

When I hung up with Stephanie, I had a good feeling that she would start spreading the story. And while I may not have been the most popular girl at our school, I think everyone at least knew me as the sweet, sheltered girl with an eccentric taste who flew under the radar and never bothered anybody. So when they all found out I had been scorned, I could win their empathy, and if that happened, I wouldn't have to push Josh away myself, which I knew I might not be capable of doing. He would be pushed away by the angry mob, with Stephanie at the helm, and maybe, just maybe, I could quietly back away during the flashy distraction.

Everybody loved a scandal, a salacious affair, and I could play the part of the jaded ex. I would do it flawlessly, and nobody would have to know what happened behind closed doors, on the long blue couch by the window while my parents were at work. Nobody would have to know that my life, my sanity, had been endangered behind a smokescreen of cold deceit, blind anger, forceful hands and sharp tongues. The venomous words and deadly threats would live in my mind alone. And I would have to relearn how to live, how to love.

The clean, unassuming girl who existed before this was gone, replaced and hardened. But I told myself that that was better than remaining captive, spending my life waiting for the next attack. If I stayed in that world where nothing was sacred, and everything was fear, where butterflies were merely jitters, and quiet panic hung thick in the static air, I would have died there, or at best, been lost forever.

I felt hopeful for the first time in months. I tried to push past the deep betrayal that was creeping in when I thought of Josh and Harper together, but this time the darkness wasn't fading when I swallowed it down, and I felt myself sinking into a starless trench. I tried swallowing again, harder this time, and shaking my head, but it didn't work.

Pull it together, I told myself. *This is a good thing. You could be near the end of this. Don't mess it up now.* But the constant tension in my muscles began to ease when I realized that I was so close to getting pulled out of the rubble instead of getting buried underneath it. And as my body started enjoying the early feelings of freedom, my mind sadly realized that with the unclenching also came the loss of my protective guard. I was no longer in survival mode. And while that should've been good news, it also meant that the scary feelings I'd so safely pushed down and tucked away to focus on making it through each day were now surfacing as my shield began melting.

I pictured Josh and Harper lying close to each other in Harper's twin bed, atop her mint green silky sheets, snuggling while they laughed about my cluelessness. I wondered if he kissed her softly. I wondered if he gently traced her body with his fingertips before they made love. I wondered if he thought of me when he touched her. Did he wish her skin was as soft as mine? Did he close his eyes and pretend it was my small waist he had his arm around? Or did he love her imperfections? Did he count her freckles and cherish her frumpy frame and flat chest? And whatever the case was, why did he choose me to hurt and her to love? The questions swirled in my head, gaining momentum as they grew and forced me to visualize the hard truths.

I tapped my fingers. I swallowed as hard as I could. I shook my head, but none of the usual tactics were working. It felt like the walls were closing and I was suddenly claustrophobic. I stood up and stumbled into the kitchen, turning on the faucet and trying to splash water on my face.

"Wake up!" I said aloud. But the inky black darkness beat through my veins, and I became completely overwhelmed by my thoughts. *He made love to her. She was good enough. You were fucked on the couch and left for dead. You were not good enough.* I became consumed.

I turned off the faucet and stared at the kitchen counter, where the wooden block of chopping knives sat, taunting me. I didn't want to hurt myself, quite the opposite. I just wanted to open my skin and let all of this poison out. I knew if I thought about it too long, I would talk myself out of it. So I grabbed the long, silver bread knife and held it to my forearm, near the elbow, and pressed down, sliding the serrated blade a few inches down my arm. I felt satisfied as I watched the ruby red blood stream out, slowly at first. I exhaled with relief and tossed the knife into the sink, running cold water against the stained metal. I held a paper towel to my arm and watched the blood as it blotted through. It wasn't painful. It was liberating.

I applied pressure to the fresh wound and pressed down until the bleeding clotted and turned to a trickle and then halted entirely. I sat down at the kitchen table and took deep breaths.

I felt high off the release it provided and lifted the paper towel to look at my work. The rough, red slash on my arm was imperfect, deep, and in the early stages of scabbing. I loved it. I loved looking at it. Finally, I had a physical manifestation for some of this darkness that made my bones ache. It was beautiful to me. I would put a bandage on it and cover myself with long sleeves before my parents got home. But until then I wanted to wear it proudly so I could look down and say to myself, *there it is, that pain and despair you felt. It's not all in your head. It's right there, I can see it.* And it made sense to me. Deep, imperfect sense.

Chapter Twenty-Seven

I knew I could count on Stephanie. Not even an hour after our conversation, I got a phone call from Ethan.

"I swear to God, I'm going to kill him," Ethan said.

"So I guess you heard ... who told you?"

"Um, I think Kyle heard it from Stephanie and he texted me, but it doesn't matter, I'm so pissed. You poor thing, you must be devastated. I knew that guy was weird. I knew he was bad news, but this is ... unforgivable."

I appreciated Ethan's anger on my behalf, but I couldn't shake an inherent frustration that quickly followed. When Josh was just the guy who Ethan watched brutalize me in the hallway, the guy who had to be physically restrained by a teacher, Ethan did little more than offer a comforting hug. But now, knowledge of the affair was widely spreading, and Josh was public enemy number one. Why was sleeping with my friend unforgivable, but the overt assault was somehow a matter I was meant to handle privately? However, if this led to Josh being out of my life, why should I care how it happened? Wasn't I still getting the result I wanted?

If Ethan knew, I wondered how long it would take for Carter to find out. Not long, I hoped. If he knew, he would hug me and hold me and tell me everything would be okay. And if Carter said everything would be okay, maybe that meant it really would be. I knew I didn't deserve any sweet gesture he would offer, but at that moment, I wanted nothing more.

When my parents got home that night, I didn't have the energy to tell them. I would eventually, or they'd find out as the news continued to spread, but I wasn't ready to have another big conversation about the betrayal. I thought it'd be nice to spend an evening away from it, where we could just talk about normal things, like college applications and what movies were coming out this weekend. And it was nice. And when I'd feel the urge to talk or think about Josh, Harper, or anything in between, I would rub my arm, even though it was hidden behind the long sleeve of a flannel shirt. I could still feel the sting from the closing wound, which would give me a twisted sense of comfort so I could continue my distraction.

The next day was the start of a weekend, which meant my parents would be home during the day. This was good because that also meant Josh wouldn't show up unannounced, but it was difficult because I had to put in extra effort to appear normal and complacent. So I was relieved that afternoon when I got a text from Carter, asking me to come over. I told myself he must know.

As I drove to Carter's house, I started getting nervous. And not my normal excited-to-see-Carter nervous, but more like what-have-I-done nervous. I knew he would find out about the affair. I had to assume everybody would find out for me to have moved forward with calling Stephanie that day. But realizing Carter would have a small peek into my distorted spectacle of a personal life was embarrassing. I wanted him to only ever think of me as this uncomplicated, serene, beautiful woman who would solely add love and light to his life, not the pathetic teenager whose boyfriend had to sleep with her homely best friend to be satisfied.

Maybe I hadn't thought this through well enough. But I reminded myself that the plan all along was to let Carter go. Even if I could become the composed, glamorous girl I convinced myself he wanted, I could never erase the fact that I was damaged goods. Certainly, Carter deserved someone who could stand up for themselves, who knew how to say no to an angry ex-boyfriend, who knew how to keep their legs closed. Carter Wells was magnificent, arresting, alluring. And I was cutting myself to cope with my dark, disturbed mind. We never had a chance. And even if we had once, it was violently extinguished that hot summer morning on the blue couch.

When I arrived at his house, I knew I shouldn't have come. The closer I got to Carter, the harder it would be to let him go. But I was selfish, and I needed to feel his safe, strong arms wrap gently around me while I rested my head in his soft, cotton hoodie.

I saw him in the living room, through the sliding glass door, so I waved and let myself in.

Before saying anything, he gave me a weak, sympathetic smile and reached for me.

I fell into him, feeling every inch of his embrace and trying to memorize the way his body felt against mine in case this was the last time I'd feel it.

He kissed the side of my head and hugged me tighter.

I felt myself getting lost, but the sting from the cut on my arm brought me back to reality as I tried to collect myself.

"Ethan texted me last night. I'm sorry about your friend," he said, still hugging me, his textured jaw resting against my head. I opened my mouth, trying to say it was okay and that I was fine, but no words came out. Instead, my throat tightened, and my chin quivered. I started crying and tried my hardest to stop.

You are embarrassing yourself, I said in my mind, humiliated. But I felt so secure with Carter, so protected, that I accidentally slipped out of my fake normalcy for a moment, which had been the only thing holding me slightly together.

"Shh, shh, you're okay. It's okay," he said, swaying back and forth as he held me.

"I'm sorry. I'm so sorry," I said between sobs, trying to wipe my face with my hands so I didn't leave stains on his red hoodie. I finally pulled back and used my sleeves to clean my cheeks and eyes. I probably looked disheveled and flustered, not peaceful and elegant like I wanted him to see me. "I'm so embarrassed." I was unable to look at him. "I didn't mean to cry, I just ... I'm so sorry."

"Andie, don't be sorry." He brought his hand to my face to wipe a new tear that was forming. "What happened was messed up, okay? You have every right to feel awful about it. I understand ... I've been cheated on before, too."

"Really?" I finally looked at him and found his eyes genuine and caring. "Why would somebody ever cheat on *you*?"

"Haha, you can ask Sloane when she gets back from Italy."

"*Sloane*? Sloane cheated on you? What happened?"

"A couple of years ago, she got drunk and slept with some guy from her art class. She confessed to it a few weeks later. It hurt like hell. It was stupid I didn't break up with her then, but I don't know, Sloane's the only girl I've ever been with. I didn't think I knew how to go through life without her. But since then, we've just continued to grow apart as we grew up, and I just ... I don't understand how you do that to someone you're supposed to love." He shrugged. "Sorry, Andie, this is *not* about me. I'm not trying to have a pity party here. I just brought it up because I wanted you to know that you're not alone. I get it. And it sucks."

I couldn't believe it. The idea of having Carter all to yourself and throwing it away by being with someone else, I hated Sloane more than ever. Carter was heaven-sent and delivered to her in this perfectly wrapped sandalwood-scented package, and she just carelessly tossed it aside and got away with it for a long time. Even if I wasn't going to end up with him, I couldn't wait for him to break up with her next month when she got home. She deserved to be alone with her stupid, perfect skin and thick, pretty hair.

"I had no idea. Wow. I can't believe you forgave Sloane."

"Ha, yeah, me either. Well, hey, it wasn't all bad. It made for a lot of good songs," he joked. I smiled. "So ... does this have something to do with why things were so weird the other day? I've been kinda worried. You just didn't seem like yourself."

I wanted to tell him that *was* the real me, though. Dark, sad, evasive. Whatever he saw in me that he found lovely and intriguing, *those* were probably the parts I was faking. But I just nodded my head. That was easier than explaining.

He hugged me again. "You're beautiful even when you're sad," he said.

But I didn't believe him. If I was beautiful and kind and interesting and all the things that Carter wanted and deserved in a girl, then how could Josh treat me the way he did? You don't hit someone who's doing everything right. You don't assault someone when they're beautiful and perfect. And you definitely don't fall in love with their best friend if they're everything you ever wanted. If Carter stayed with me for long enough, he'd figure that out for himself, too. So I couldn't let him.

Chapter Twenty-Eight

Weeks had passed since Josh and Harper's affair was exposed, and true to her word, Stephanie had done her part in not letting them live it down. They had become outcasts, pariahs. Even Kid A was split, Nicole and a few of her most loyal cronies stuck by Josh, but to my surprise, most of Kid A sympathized with me and wanted nothing to do with him. One of them even likened the situation to kicking a puppy. It was the first time I had been grateful to have such a goody-goody reputation. The sympathy came much easier.

Josh tried contacting me once, but when I told Stephanie, she wrote this note and left it on the windshield of his car:

Josh,

If you reach out to Andrea Cavanaugh even one more time, if you so much as even text to ask about the weather, things will get a lot worse for you than they already have. Your parents will find out about all the stuff you smoke. Yes, I know about that. Everybody knows about that. And if they don't care, I'll call the police and show them where you and Nicole get high. And you will get caught. And you will get arrested. So stay the fuck away from Andrea.

Love,

Stephanie :)

It was pretty incredible, and he seemed to take it seriously because I hadn't heard from him since she left him that note. I felt terrible that I'd spent the last few years getting so close to Harper while I pushed aside my real friends like Stephanie, who had been there all along. But I was thankful that she didn't hold it against me. Stephanie didn't know it, but she had saved my life.

I'd been trying to keep Carter at arm's length, but it was hard. I kept slipping on my vow to let him go. When I'd be alone with my thoughts, I'd remind myself why it was important and how I was just dragging out the inevitable by letting him continue to think I was an average, well-adjusted person. But then I'd see him and melt under his big, dark eyes and tell myself I'd try again next time. I was weak, and he was gorgeous. It was a dangerous combination.

Then one night, my parents took me out to dinner at the country club. I never liked going there. I had to dress up, and the food wasn't great, but it was their favorite, so I went along.

After we had ordered, I felt my heart jump when my mother looked up at someone apparently standing behind me.

"Donna! How are you?" she cheerily said.

It was Josh's mom.

I turned around in my chair and forced a smile.

Please just say hi and leave, I begged her in my mind. I still hadn't told my parents about Josh and Harper.

"Hi, Cavanaughs," Mrs. McMillan said. "I saw you guys from across the room and wanted to come over and formally apologize to Andrea for my son's behavior."

I closed my eyes, dreading where the conversation was going, knowing my parents would be confused and then angry I hadn't told them. But I couldn't stop her.

"Andrea." She looked directly at me. "I am sorry. Really and truly. This Harper Cooley is over at our house every day now, and it makes me miss you more than ever. You've always been so lovely, and I noticed a significant change for the better in Josh when you two were together. Now it's … well, it's challenging."

"Andrea, what is she talking about?" my dad asked.

"It's nothing," I said quickly.

"Oh, I'm sorry," Mrs. McMillan said awkwardly. "I just assumed Andrea told you about Josh and Harper. But oh well, what can you do, teenagers in love think they know everything. Boys will be boys," she said with a light laugh. I felt my parents' eyes on me. "Sorry to interrupt. Anyway, enjoy your dinner," Mrs. McMillan said, sensing she'd said too much, before walking back to her table.

"Andrea, is that true? Josh and Harper are dating now?" my mom asked seriously. I nodded. "Why didn't you tell us? That's awful. You must be heartbroken."

"No, no," I stammered. "It's fine."

"But Harper is your best friend, that's just ... not what best friends do."

"We're not exactly friends anymore..." I started squirming in my seat. This wasn't how I'd hoped to tell them.

"Well, don't let some boy ruin a good friendship," my dad naively offered.

"It's not just that," I said. "They've *been* together since, well, since the beginning of last school year, I guess. So like, the majority of my relationship with Josh, too."

"So they cheated?" my mom whispered angrily.

I nodded again.

"That's terrible, Andie, I'm just ... I'm so sorry. Why didn't you tell us?" my mom said, the guilt dripping off her words. I had never intended to make them feel bad about this, which I think is why I'd kept it from them for so long. And then the longer I waited, the more the "why didn't you tell us sooner" argument was validated, and the worse I felt. But now, at least this part, was out in the open. I appreciated the well-deserved sympathy I got from my friends and classmates and even from Carter, but I hated making my parents feel sorry for me because I knew they were quick to blame themselves, and I wanted to shield them from that, especially since I was the only one deserving of blame. This happened in spite of them, not because of them, but I knew they would struggle to see it that way.

Feeling guilty and more uncomfortable by the minute, I excused myself to the bathroom. I figured if I was gone a few moments, I could re-enter and hopefully change the conversation topic more naturally as I sat back down.

But as I swung the door open to the bathroom, I let out an internal groan when I saw Donna standing in front of the floor-length mirror, reapplying her burgundy lipstick.

"Andrea! Honey, I'm sorry if I put my foot in my mouth over there. But it is really good to see you."

My shoulders tensed. "It's okay."

"Honey, I'm glad you came in here. I was hoping we'd have a chance to talk."

I felt nauseous. I didn't want to speak to her or hear anything she had to say. Donna was a pleasant enough woman but just looking at her made my skin crawl because her eyes resembled her son's so intricately. "I just ... I'm really worried about Josh. I think he's falling into a bad crowd. He was so happy when you two were together, and now he's just getting into trouble. Someone even told me..." Her voice cracked, and she bit her lip, trying not to cry. She cleared her throat. "Someone said he's doing drugs." Her voice turned to a whisper.

"I don't know," was all I could say.

Donna was correct in her assumptions, and she

should be worried about him. But she was his mother. I was his ex-girlfriend who he continued to berate and threaten even after our relationship ended. This was not for me to get involved in.

"I just ... do you think ... do you think you can talk to him?" she asked meekly, tears forming above her smudged eyeliner.

I was so angry that she would put this responsibility on me. Initially, I felt sorry for her, but I had to push that aside if I were to survive. And I didn't just go through all of this to get sucked back in.

"No, I ... I'm sorry, but no." I started backing away toward the door.

"I can't get through to him. It would mean so much."

"No, I'm sorry," I said again as I opened the door and slipped out, hearing her call my name from behind me. As I walked down the hallway back into the dining room, I pictured Donna left alone in that bathroom. I knew how she felt. Isolated, broken, devastated. But this was a life sentence for her. I did my time, and I had to save myself. If I tried to help her, we would both end up stuck. My heart broke more with each step I took away from that door, but I told myself I was doing the right thing. Perhaps it was the selfish move, and I'd never been terribly good at being selfish, but slowly walking away from that bathroom felt like I was running for my life. And I couldn't look back now.

Even though I was rattled, I sat back down at the table with my parents and tried to change the subject cheerily. We didn't speak about Josh or Harper anymore that evening. But that's how things usually worked in my family. When it came to love, there was more than enough to pass around, but when a hard truth or negative emotion was uncovered, it was quickly kicked under the rug, and everyone uncomfortably pretended it had never happened. My parents were joyful, generous people who worked hard and loved me. I was lucky, and I knew that. I didn't take it for granted. But the glass was *so* half-full that we sometimes drowned ourselves in it.

That night, as I got ready for bed, my mom walked into my room and sat on the end of my bed. She didn't have to say anything—I could read her face. She was probably thinking, "We used to be so close, when did she stop coming to me with these things?" and "If I didn't work so much, I could've been there for her." I knew she thought that because I had thought that at one point, too. But I also knew deep down that I was worth leaving. And punishing. And threatening. And cheating on. And until I could figure out what was so wrong with me, what about me was so hard to love, then I couldn't blame anyone but myself. Not my mother, not my father, not even Josh. I could've said no.

"Honey, I don't know what to say. I just want you to know you can talk to me," my mom said softly, choosing her words carefully.

"I know, Mom." I sat down next to her. "I'm sorry I didn't tell you sooner. I guess it was just kinda embarrassing."

"Nobody should treat you like that." She put her arm around me.

"Thanks," I said, knowing she was wrong.

My dad walked into the doorway.

"Karen, are you coming to bed?" he asked my mom. She nodded and went to stand up. As I looked at my dad standing there, fighting how uncomfortable he was, I tried to picture what he was thinking. His hands were toying with the loose hem of the old college sweatshirt he wore to bed, and his eyes couldn't seem to focus on one thing.

It had always been an unspoken rule that my mother was the one to talk to me about boys, dating, and sex. My dad was there as our protector, coach, and occasional comic relief, always quick with a joke or a lesson. So the fact that he knew about this teenage love triangle forced him to look at me as more than just his little girl. I was now a young woman who was also someone's ex-girlfriend, somebody's scorned lover, and that was hard for him to accept. So he was trying not to. He wanted to swallow it away, which I so deeply understood.

At that moment, as I watched his big, rough hands fiddle with the fabric on his shirt and his sweet, sad eyes dart around the room, I felt more connected to him than I ever had. Even though I was the cause of his discomfort, I understood it so clearly and recognized the kindred nature in which he tried to avoid it.

In an unexpected fearless moment, I stood up and floated toward him.

I just want my daddy, I kept repeating in my head. He had no idea the hell I had been through, and if he knew it would crush him. But in that instant, it felt like maybe we could both get what we wanted. We could hug and pretend like I *was* his little girl again. Back to a time when my dad, strong and valiant, was the only man in my life, and therefore nothing and nobody could hurt me. I wanted to go back there, even if just for a second, and I felt like he did, too, so I reached out and hugged him, burying my face in his chest and waiting for him to return my embrace.

But he didn't. He softly patted the back of my arms and backed away. "Good night, Andrea," he said as he turned around and disappeared into his bedroom, my mom close behind.

I stayed frozen for a moment, my arms still

outstretched before I realized what had happened. I was no longer the girl from the photos my father had framed on his office desk. I was damaged, and even he saw that. It wasn't just my secret anymore. It was written all over me.

I slumped down on my bed and tried to put my thoughts together, but there were too many. I pressed on the healing cut on my arm, but it didn't hurt anymore. The scab was almost gone.

Frustrated, I dug my fingernails into where it had been and scratched and pulled until I felt the familiar stinging sensation. When I saw specks of blood rise to the surface, I felt better. I quietly walked to the bathroom where I ran it under cold water before applying a new bandage.

When I sat back down and looked at it, I was satisfied. Flawed, broken skin. It was fitting. At least now I looked the part.

Chapter Twenty-Nine

When my phone rang at 2 AM that night, I woke up with a pang of terror in my chest.

I was sure it was Josh. He was probably drunk or high or lonely or angry or all of the above. I knew he couldn't let this go. But when I saw Carter's name on the screen as it vibrated, I quickly answered, relieved but confused.

"Carter?" I sleepily asked as I rubbed my eyes, trying to pull myself into the moment.

"Andie, I'm sorry I'm calling so late." His voice was hushed, but he sounded excited.

"What's going on? Are you okay?"

"I'm ... great actually." I could hear the smile in his voice. "I know it's 2 AM. but it's 8 AM in Rome."

"Okay..." I still didn't understand how that was relevant.

"I just hung up with Sloane. It's over, Andie. I'm not waiting for her to come back. I can't."

I had trouble thinking of words.

"I ... are you sure? I mean ... what?" It was all I could get out as I tried to piece together what he was saying.

"I want to be with you. Not Sloane. Not anybody else. And I realized I was waiting to break up with her in person because I thought that would be the right thing to do. But when has Sloane ever done the right thing by me? Ya know? I just ... I couldn't wait anymore."

I felt my breathing grow shallow as I tried to wrap my tired mind around what he was saying. Carter Wells wanted to be with me. There was not a universe where that fully made sense.

"Are you ... are you sure?"

"Am I sure? Haha, of course. I can't get you out of my head. I'm crazy about you. I thought that was pretty obvious."

"But ... there's so much you don't know," I said, remembering that this could never work. I'd already been through this in my head. He would never feel this way if he knew the real me. If he knew the damaged, weak-willed girl who only had a decent body because she threw up her food due to the crippling anxiety she felt from being tormented by someone who was supposed to have loved her. If he knew the pathetic, meek teenager who had just reopened the cut on her arm because she couldn't cope with the way her parents looked at her now. That was the girl he was "crazy about?" No, that was the girl you left. The girl you forced a smile at and feigned politeness so you could talk to her cooler, hotter friends.

"There's a lot you don't know about me, too," he said. But that was different. Any skeletons Carter had in his closet would likely come out in charming stories where he created some artistic masterpiece as a result of. "But we'll get to know each other better. I want to know everything about you." He sounded so sure, so relieved, and his voice comforted me like a warm, velvety robe.

"Andie? You there?" he asked after a long pause. I wanted to tell him that I would adore him sincerely and intensely, with my whole heart, until the day he inevitably met somebody better, prettier, more sophisticated and less complicated. I wanted to tell him that he was all I thought about when my mind wasn't consumed with fear and flashbacks. I wanted him to know how effortlessly gorgeous he was, how impeccably talented and just how devoutly flawless he was in my eyes, in everyone's eyes. But I was struck by this nagging reminder in my head—*if you care about Carter, you won't put him through this.* I was a hurricane, leaving desolation in my path, and Carter was ... well, he was the sun. I couldn't look at him for long without having to shield my eyes.

I knew the next year was going to be a mess of dealing with the cluster of emotions that were burning just under the surface of my skin. Plus, I'd have to spend the year avoiding Josh in the hallways and coping with the paralyzing fear that would come every time I did see him.

"You're making me nervous ... please say something," he said.

"I'm just ... scared."

"Scared of what?"

"Disappointing you. I'm not good at this. And I'm afraid you're going to figure that out sooner than later."

"Well, we'll never know unless we try, right?"

I could hear that half-smile come through the phone and just picturing his perfectly sculpted face feeling relaxed and optimistic gave me a little peace, a little strength. I bit my lip hard while I thought.

"Come on, Andrea. Just close your eyes and jump with me," he whispered excitedly.

"But what if it doesn't work out?" I could feel the fear creeping back in.

"Well ... I've always believed that the hopeless romantics are the first to be redeemed, even if it all comes crashing down because they were brave enough to love vulnerably and fearlessly."

"Forgiven are the starry-eyed..." I said, trailing off as I remembered his apropos lyric, a smile starting to form on my pale, weary face.

"Where'd you hear that? Some great, wise philosopher?" he joked, with a small laugh.

"Yeah, something like that."

So I jumped. Selfishly and brilliantly, I jumped

in, with the intention of never looking back. But I knew better. I knew I would be looking back for a long, long time. I couldn't erase what had been done to me or what I had caused. But in that one, pure moment, my starry-eyes were clouded with hope, so I ran with it.

I knew it could end in misery. I knew I could be left broken hearted and shattered, and I knew he could find out all my secrets and find me untouchable and even forgettable. But I also knew that there was a chance we could be happy. There was a chance we could be left breathless and intertwined. And that, to me, was worth the risk. Even Josh hadn't completely erased that optimism from my soul, though it wasn't without a fight. So as I vowed to take this step with Carter, regardless of how uncertain or fraught with danger it could be. I thought for the first time in a long time that maybe, just maybe, one day I would be okay. And maybe I would even find a little forgiveness along the way.

The next morning, I was wrought with hope and had butterflies in my stomach. It had been so long since I'd felt anything other than the nauseating turns of dark anxiety, so this change was exhilarating. I felt alive for a moment, remembering Carter's words from last night.

I reached for my phone and saw two texts from him waiting for me.

Carter: I'm so excited, Andie.

Carter: Call me when you wake up. I want to see you. Let's hang out and make this real.

I closed my eyes and exhaled, allowing this rush to wash over me. I took it in for a brief moment before I had to reenter my real world of uncertainty and fear. I started drafting a text back to Carter but stopped abruptly when I remembered something. Hope. I had stashed it away in the back of my bedside drawer in the off-chance I'd ever be ready or willing or alive enough to use it.

Rummaging through my drawer, I found the familiar lavender business card beneath some hair ties, pens, and scribbled notes and pulled it out, studying it on my bed.

"Stacey Hawthorne, LCSW" The phone number stared back at me from the thick, creased card. If I called her, she would probably dismiss my story and roll her eyes, or awkwardly lecture me and scoff at the details. But ... what if she didn't? I was drunk on optimism and I dialed the number before I could talk myself out of it.

It started ringing and I almost hung up.

"Stacey Hawthorne's office," a friendly, female voice said on the other end. "Hello?" she asked again as I sat there silent, realizing I had no idea what to say.

"Sorry ... I ... um ... my name is ... I got this card from..." I stammered. Why had I called? I immediately felt my face flushing.

"It's okay, honey," the woman said warmly. "My name is Abby. I'm Stacey's receptionist. Are you a patient?"

"No!" I blurted the word out quickly.

"Okay, no problem. Did you want to schedule some time to talk to Stacey?" Abby asked kindly.

"Maybe?" I said, rolling my eyes at how stupid I probably sounded.

Abby asked a few basic questions I could give easy one-word answers to, like my name, my age, my date of birth, but then she asked if I'd be paying through insurance or cash and I choked. I'd had some money saved up from work but not a lot, and if I used insurance, I'd have to explain it to my parents since I was on their plan. But maybe that wasn't the worst idea in the world? I wouldn't have to tell them everything. I could even just say I needed help mentally preparing for college or something, and knowing them, there wouldn't be additional questions. Or ... I *could* tell them everything.

Even if they did nothing, even if they refused to accept my story for what it was, I could let some of this poison out of my body if I said the facts out loud.

In a sudden bout of unrecognizable confidence, I told Abby I'd be using insurance. She set up a time for me the following week to come in and talk to Stacey Hawthorne, LCSW (which, she nicely explained, stood for "licensed clinical social worker"). I hung up the phone and finished my text to Carter.

Me: I'm excited too. Come over at noon?

He responded with a thumbs up emoji and I flopped back onto my bed.

What am I doing? I kept asking my racing mind. But something inside of me wanted to fight. Love existed, I was sure of it, and maybe that was worth fighting for if I couldn't fight for myself.

My bedroom door opened a bit and my mom poked her head in.

"Oh good. You're awake. I just wanted to let you know I'm leaving for work now. See you at dinner. Call if you need anything, okay?"

"Okay," I responded, and she began to shut the door.

"Wait!" I pleaded.

She reopened the door slightly and pushed her head back through with questioning eyes.

"Can we talk later? Tonight maybe?" I asked quietly.

"Sure, sweetie, of course. Is everything okay?"

"Yeah. No. Kind-of. I don't know. I think it will be…" I said, knowing the lingering mystery was difficult to understand.

She squinted at me, trying to read my face. "Do you … need to talk now?" she asked awkwardly.

"No, sorry, later is fine. It's fine, Mom, I swear," I

said, trying to minimize the impact of what I knew was going to be a heavy conversation.

"Okay..." She trailed off. "Just ... take care today, Andie. We'll talk more later." She closed the door softly behind her and I bit my lip until I couldn't feel it anymore. I was going to do this. I was going to talk about it. And maybe nothing would change. But maybe everything would change. I couldn't erase what had happened, I never would. But maybe I didn't have to live like this every day. Maybe Carter could see beyond the damage if I let it out? Maybe Josh would leave me alone if I exposed the truth as I knew it? Or maybe it'd all come crashing down around me, but that was a familiar feeling that I wasn't scared of anymore. I could deal with desolation, I knew bleakness and despair like the back of my hand, and I was still alive. If I could learn how to live in that world, maybe I could let someone teach me how to live in the other world, where the starry-eyed really were forgiven and the lovers really did prosper. I didn't know if it was possible, but for the first time in as long as I could remember, the harrowing future I'd assumed was inevitable didn't feel so certain anymore.

The End

CHRISTINE DORÉ MILLER

Evernight Teen ®

www.evernightteen.com

Made in the USA
Middletown, DE
08 May 2019